Gnomes of Lychford

ALSO BY PAUL CORNELL

THE WITCHES OF LYCHFORD SERIES
Witches of Lychford
The Lost Child of Lychford
A Long Day in Lychford
The Lights Go Out in Lychford
Last Stand in Lychford

THE SHADOW POLICE SERIES
London Falling
The Severed Streets
Who Killed Sherlock Holmes?

Rosebud
Chalk
British Summertime
Something More
A Better Way to Die (collection)

GNOMES OF LYCHFORD

PAUL CORNELL

TOR PUBLISHING GROUP
NEW YORK

This is a work of fiction. All of the characters, organizations, and events portrayed in this novella are either products of the author's imagination or are used fictitiously.

GNOMES OF LYCHFORD

Copyright © 2025 by Paul Cornell

All rights reserved.

A Tordotcom Book
Published by Tom Doherty Associates / Tor Publishing Group
120 Broadway
New York, NY 10271

www.torpublishinggroup.com

Tor® is a registered trademark of Macmillan Publishing Group, LLC.

EU Representative: Macmillan Publishers Ireland Ltd, 1st Floor, The Liffey Trust Centre, 117–126 Sheriff Street Upper, Dublin 1, DO1 YC43

The Library of Congress Cataloging-in-Publication Data
is available upon request.

ISBN 978-1-250-38827-8 (trade paperback)
ISBN 978-1-250-38828-5 (ebook)

The publisher of this book does not authorize the use or reproduction of any part of this book in any manner for the purpose of training artificial intelligence technologies or systems. The publisher of this book expressly reserves this book from the Text and Data Mining exception in accordance with Article 4(3) of the European Union Digital Single Market Directive 2019/790.

Our books may be purchased in bulk for specialty retail/wholesale, literacy, corporate/premium, educational, and subscription box use. Please contact MacmillanSpecialMarkets@macmillan.com.

First Edition: 2025

Printed in the United States of America

10 9 8 7 6 5 4 3 2 1

For the patrons, proprietor, and bar staff of the Railway Inn, Fairford.

Gnomes of Lychford

Prologue

IN THE PAST FEW YEARS, life in the little Cotswolds market town of Lychford had become a lot more complicated.

Much of this complication had happened all at once, in that extraordinary half hour when a shower of rain had given everyone who'd got the water on their skin the ability to see magic and monsters and much else that was terrifying and wondrous—all of which was, apparently, real. All that stuff, the inhabitants of Lychford had subsequently been told, had in the past been noticed, confronted, and defeated by a select few. Now it had become everyone's problem. Which was... better? Possibly? At any rate, everyone now had a story about how their cat or lottery ticket or uncle had gone missing back in the day, and how that all now made so much more sense.

Another great dollop of complication had arrived with what everyone now tended to call "the incident," that time with the, err, angel and oh dear perhaps Satan, and you know, the end of the world.

These complications were reflected, as a lot of local

life was, in the conduct of the meetings of the Lychford Town Council.

Loz Watson, the town clerk, had been in the role for nearly two decades, and part of her was sort of pleased that her job had, in the last year or so, taken a pronounced turn toward the inexplicable. Another, bigger part of her was absolutely bloody appalled by it. "Any other business?" (which was what the Chair said once they'd got through the agenda at every weekly council meeting) had previously been her favorite phrase. It had meant that in five minutes they could all go down the pub. Now it was an invitation to partake in mystery and imagination, a phrase akin to "once upon a time..." and it regularly signalled the start of three hours of surreal group therapy.

The looks on the faces of her fellow councillors at this particular meeting told her they had all started to feel the same way. Apart from Jim, of course. Jim was the sort of older gentleman who favored russet trousers as if that made him a bit of a rebel and wore his bushy antenna-like eyebrows and sprouting ear hair like badges of pride. At this precise moment he was doing that most awful of things in the moment after "any other business": he was grasping the lapels of his tired old jacket. Oh, he had other business all right. "Madam Chairwoman..." he began.

Loz minuted it on her tablet as "Chair" as said Chair literally rolled her eyes.

"... I have tried to deal with this situation. I have tried to find common ground with it. But it is with much sorrow that I now see no alternative but the ultimate sanction. I wish to have it recorded in the minutes that I'm against."

"Against what?" said the Chair, Carrie Anne Christopher. Her voice had inclined, as it always did in reply to Jim, toward the full *Importance of Being Earnest*. She had recently left the Lychford Festival Committee in order to join the council and had looked vaguely suspicious when most of the existing members had immediately encouraged her to become Chair. Now she was clearly discovering what all that had been about.

"Against all these changes. Against the so-called magic. And the strangers. And the way our lives have been turned upside down. And how none of it has done a damn thing to fix the potholes."

Loz kept her usual calm expression on her face as she tapped in the exact words, because Jim always read the minutes, and would send her notes. She had been recording his thoughts for the best part of her two decades, and though she had been tempted, and never more so than now, she had never added an adverb of any sort. She was starting to feel that alone should put her in line for a

CBE. How Jim could refer to seeing strange beasts flapping their way overhead, the woods lighting up like a celestial rock concert, and the random appearance in their town of everything from a rain of frogs to baked goods which hummed Gilbert and Sullivan as "so-called..." Well, hers was not to reason why. And "strangers" was one hell of a way to refer to the weird beings that every few weeks ventured into the town, sometimes at night, sometimes in the broad daylight on market day. Unless Jim was referring to the tourists from Bristol and London, and dear God, Glastonbury, who'd heard about the impossible things that were whispered to have happened here and came to seek them out while not buying anything. Loz thought that what the new "Wise Woman" Autumn Blunstone and her friend the vicar Lizzie Blackmore and that new one behind the counter at the magic shop, Zoya Boyko, said was simply true: that Lychford lay on the borders of many mystical realms, accessed through the woods, and that those borders were now wide open. She could understand someone who hadn't felt the rain still not getting that. But Jim had been standing there outside the chip shop in that downpour with his eyes bulging out of their sockets. It was perhaps more a matter of perceived duty for him, she thought. It was as if he felt who he was demanded he be angry at anything new. The rain and all that had come after had been just too much of an affront to his aging self-image. It had, it seemed, put a sort of reality other than his own at the centre of the world. And that would never do.

"I'm not sure," fellow Councillor Sunil Mehra, another new recruit in the wake of "the incident," carefully began, "how one can be 'against' something that was literally the weather. It's just how things are now."

"To be fair," said Jackie Parker, who ran the nail salon, "Jim's against a lot that's just how things are now."

"Sunil, my friend," said Jim, "you are not an objective commentator, considering your . . . relationship with the late so-called 'Wise Woman' whose shenanigans with the so-called supernatural started all this—"

"Before you say one word about Judith," said Sunil, sounding dangerously mild, "consider how often she saved your behind and that of everyone else in this town and the world. And the great service you've always had at my restaurants. Previously."

"Everybody!" shouted Carrie Anne Christopher. "Please! We're only two minutes into Any Other Business. Your protest at the rain has been minuted, Jim"—Loz allowed herself a little smile at that—"and we are moving on. Anyone else?"

"I think this situation has a lot of upsides," said Matt Coomby. Matt was a Liberal Democrat who'd moved into one of the more upmarket New Builds a few weeks before the rain. He'd been in London on business for the downpour, and so hadn't been affected himself, but his partner and their toddler had been, and ever since he'd been finding bloody upsides about the situation on a regular basis. "We need to think about making the most of our tourist potential, give those who come to see spooky stuff a focus, so they don't go wandering about with the wrong expectations."

"You mean... create a place for them to mill about aimlessly that actually makes the town some money?" Carrie Anne Christopher sounded as if, to her surprise, one of her fellow councillors had actually had a good idea.

"If you want," said Matt with a shrug. "Also, more electric car points."

It was at that moment that Dave the Mayor entered. Dave Awlish was a builder, with the slim muscular body typical of his trade, the sort of physique that seemed weirdly impervious to beer. Loz always perked up when he made his entrance. He was actually meant to be here for the whole meeting, but with only a few weeks of his term left to go, he'd started to arrive later and later. His rather wonderful shoulders looked to be carrying a greater burden with every passing week. "Sorry I'm late," he said, his accent redolent of the town, the countryside around it, and the particular working-class wealth of the subculture of builders who made Lychford their home. "Are we in . . . any other business?"

Carrie Anne Christopher looked daggers at him. "Oh we so are. There are things you need to sign off on, Mr. Mayor, Jim is protesting at the weather, and Matthew has had a good idea."

"Oh ah," said Dave, sitting down with a guilty schoolboy look. "So what's the general feeling about the gnomes?" The meeting fell entirely silent. The councillors looked at each other in puzzlement. Loz wondered if and how she should record this eerie moment in the minutes. Dave's expression grew solemn. "My fellow councillors," he said, "has nobody mentioned the gnome in the room?" And he nodded toward a corner.

Everyone looked over to the corner where indeed there stood a gnome. It had in its hands a tiny notepad and seemed to have been caught in the act of taking its own set of minutes. It looked as surprised at having been noticed as Loz was at its existence, presence, and the fact that up until now none of them had noticed it. "Oh," it said, "please, don't let me stop you."

1

OWEN TRAFALGAR WAS THE OWNER and landlord of the Station Inn in Lychford, and the owner of a couple more gastropubs in villages where they were both the only local business and the only source of parking difficulties. His life was largely spent on his phone, often while standing in crowded car parks, and when he wasn't doing that, he was snatching moments at his riverside home with his husband, Tobin, who was something in the City and on a weekly commute. They had a pet tortoise called Pie. All that meant that, oddly for a landlord, he actually enjoyed those rare occasions when he was serving behind the bar at the Station.

Usually.

This evening, however, he was staring at Councillor Matt Coomby over a pint of Acid Biker Jolly IPA with a gathering mixture of horror and incredulity. "You've done what?"

"I've invited the *Unworldly* podcast to visit Lychford. They're very interested. And they need somewhere to stay, and I thought, since we're on the same side when it comes to bringing tourists into town—"

"What's this now?" said Mick the mechanic, from just down the bar, where he and Paul the builder had been propped every Thursday since an altercation with their last local over having too many Americans in. Mick especially had history with the weird happenings in this town, having, at the moment of greatest peril, when the world was in jeopardy, given the vicar a lift in his truck. That had now become, for him, a full-fledged anecdote. Paul's party piece, on the other hand, was his adventures with a metal detector. He had a couple of pieces in museums and could be relied upon to put a Roman coin in someone's hand if there was a lull in conversation. Some of his collection, he reported, now shone with weirdness and felt so haunted that he'd started to sell it off on eBay, Autumn Blunstone, the new Wise Woman, having first taken a look to make sure there was nothing malign he might be passing on to the unwary. These two stalwarts were typical of the Lychford old guard's reaction to the strangeness: it had unnerved and changed them, made them feel vulnerable, but it had also strengthened them and given them new purpose. These guys tended to assume they were part of the conversation if it was anywhere along this stretch of wood, and Owen felt they had a perfect right to feel that and was glad of their intervention now. Local people, he'd had to point out to the first manager he'd appointed here after he'd taken over, were a feature, not a bug. The stereotype in town was that the new, flashier people, those from the high-end families in the New Builds, hadn't been in the rain and hadn't experienced "the incident." Owen knew that to be only about half true. He tried to steer the conversation in his bar away from that assumption, because it was hard on those older local folk who didn't tend to go out in any sort of rain, and thus didn't share in what was quickly becoming a badge of community. Also, he himself wanted to be part of that community, and he hadn't experienced the rain.

"A podcast," said Matt. "About unexplained happenings, like ghosts and UFOs. It's also on Radio 4."

"Oh ah," said Paul. "And what would they want with us?"

Matt paused for a moment, as if trying to formulate a calm response. Owen recalled how Paul had been caught in "the rain" while in the garden of his former local, or at least that was how Mick told the story. He'd started to yell "Look at the sky!" over and over until Mick had slapped him. "They're interested," Matt said finally, "in our . . . unusual creatures. You know, like the gnomes."

Paul looked suddenly shocked. He put down his pint. Mick put a cautioning hand on his shoulder, but he shrugged it off. "Now you listen to me," he said. "When I go on a job in Lechlade or Cirencester, I always get people asking if what they say about Lychford is true. Because you know what they think of us? They think we're nutters. Oh"—he glanced at Linda behind the bar, who had ADHD—"no offense."

"None taken," said Linda, who often used that word about herself. "And I agree, I've changed where I'm from on all the dating sites. I get some right weirdos." She glanced at Meg with the tattoos beside her. "No offense."

"At any rate," said Paul before Meg could reply, obviously worried about getting caught in some endless loop of vaguely understood social anxiety, "I tell 'em it's all put on. And I don't want to have someone come here and say to Radio 4 and all the other podcast wankers that in this town we wander about screaming at stuff they can't see." The look of someone who'd done exactly that passed over his countenance. "This place"—he indicated the bar—"may have a theme park these days where the beer should be"—by which he meant the range of draft designer IPAs—"but Owen keeps the Guinness on for us two, and he's a good sort for someone who can't see the weird shit, and we don't want this place spoilt by a lot of London fuckwits."

"None taken," said Owen, maybe a bit too quickly. "And yeah, I agree. Obviously, Matt, your guest can stay here, but I'm not admitting to him there's anything supernatural going on." There was a noise of general agreement from all around the bar.

Matt looked around, stunned. "I thought—"

"And," continued Paul, "there's one thing above all we won't be mentioning to him." He actually stepped forward and put his finger under Matt's nose. "In this town, we do *not* talk about the gnomes."

The Reverend Lizzie Blackmore of St. Martin's church, Lychford, was lying on her vicarage sofa, staring at the ceiling, panicking.

She wasn't panicking about anything in particular. Which was bloody annoying. The anxiety had started more than a year ago, just after Russia had invaded Ukraine. It had arrived in waves, reacting to the routine of a week by making her think about the worst possible consequences of every single event. She had printed out the wrong hymns for Mr. Gregson's funeral and had had to run back to the Vicarage as the mourners were arriving: oh no, everyone was going to hate her. Her favorite brand of flavored coffee had been discontinued: oh no, her tastes must be so weird, and how would she live without it? The human race was heading for extinction because of climate change and every single action humanity took seemed to make things worse: oh no, that was . . .

as bad as it seemed, actually. And it woke her up at night and made her pray and pray, too hard, too demanding.

The people who said shit like "your faith must be such a comfort" had no bloody idea what faith was.

Plus, of course, all that "oh no" now had a magical dimension. She had actually asked her dear friend Autumn, at one point of enormous fight or flight, if she couldn't use magic to fix climate change. Autumn had said, "Well done, that's my quota of being asked that question fulfilled for another week, and no, because: magic costs! I do not have enough blood or souls or putative firstborn children handy to even begin to do that, not that I would sacrifice anything I didn't own, before you ask! And hello, good morning, by the way. God, what is up with you these days?"

Lizzie, not being able to help herself, had deflected the whole matter of what was up with her to the question of whether Autumn had meant that she and Luke were thinking about having children, and Autumn had at that point, as Lizzie knew she would, deflected back by saying she still had some of that foul hazelnut and marshmallow coffee Lizzie liked.

She hadn't told Autumn about her anxiety. She hadn't told her best friend about much of anything that was important to her lately. She had made the mistake, on the evening of Autumn and Luke's wedding, when up late having a whiskey with Zoya, of admitting her own sexuality. Or her own sort-of sexuality? What she took to be her sexuality? What she now really had trouble facing up to because it was mostly about Autumn... and sometimes about Brie Larson... but mostly about Autumn? Maybe that was why she'd started panicking soon after. And that was ridiculous, because what was to be done? Autumn and Luke were great together, were happy together, and Lizzie refused to be jealous about that. She saw jealousy in the distance of her mind and she absolutely would not let herself go there, because that was self-harm, that was something that would eat her up, that was sin.

What wasn't a sin was fancying women. Her belief system said nothing about that, because Christ had said nothing about that, and being omnipotent, if he'd wanted to, he would have. She'd fancied women even when she'd been with Joe, though it had taken her decades to realize that. Given the existence of Ryan Gosling, she supposed she was bi, not gay, but... gah. All of it. Just gah. Maybe the knowledge that even among her lovely parishioners there were a handful who would object was what had unconsciously pushed her toward panic?

Gah.

She began the process recommended by one of the three meditation apps she'd bought and given up on, breathing in for three seconds, holding it, out for three seconds, while building in her mind the shape of calm. If calm were a building, what sort of building would it be? Having done this for several months now, Lizzie had a pretty good idea of that building in her mind's eye: strong and steadfast and undemanding. And entirely unlike any building in Lychford, where everyone wanted something from her all the time.

The doorbell rang, which was kind of a relief from the new wave of anxiety that had broken her reverie. She got up and made her way to the hall, controlling her breathing.

On the doorstep stood a young man and woman, looking expectantly and slightly nervously at her, as if *she* was the one who'd just rung *their* doorbell. "Hi," said the man. "Are we early?"

"No, no, do come in, would you like a cup of tea?" Lizzie ushered them into her study, hoping at some point they would tell her who they were and what this was about.

"Great to meet you last Sunday," said the woman, who seemed a bit more socially tuned in and was clearly wondering if Lizzie needed reminding. "When we came to see the church. Because we want to get married in it?"

Lizzie was relieved that she now remembered who they were. She pointed at the woman like she'd got the answer right in charades. "You're Winnie and Brandon, and you've changed your hair and he's wearing a suit for some reason."

"Well," said Brandon, "you know, formalities. And yes please to that tea."

"So, we're new to the area," said Winnie, a while later, drinking her tea. "We live in Cirencester, but we were driving around here and we saw your church, and... well, it's idyllic, isn't it?"

"It's a very idyllic sort of... quite demanding building," said Lizzie, still doing her best not to pant, her anxiety making her hands shake on her tea mug.

"Only," added Brandon, leaning forward as if this was the difficult bit, "we then... started to hear about Lychford. About, you know..."

"The weird stuff," said Lizzie. "Which is absolutely not real."

"Well no," said Winnie, "of course not. Only, people seem to think it is, and sometimes they seem to say and do things about it that are... not being funny, but quite weird, and we decided we were going to say to you in advance—"

"—we don't want any weirdness at our wedding," finished Brandon.

"Oh, of course not!" Lizzie managed a smile as she had to put down the rattling tea mug. "It'll all go completely normally, I promise. There is absolutely nothing in this town which could disrupt it in any way. Ever."

When they left, Lizzie closed the door very gently behind them and then leaned on it.

There were so many aspects of her life about which she could no longer tell the truth. At least, not to many people.

She was about to give the meditation another go when the doorbell rang again. Thinking it was Winnie and Brandon back to add some further worrying detail to their impending ceremony, she opened the door only to find herself looking at nothing. There was nobody there.

"Down here," sighed a small voice.

She looked down.

On the Vicarage doorstep stood three gnomes. They had in their hands what looked like leaflets.

"Oh," she said. "Hello."

"Good evening," said the one that seemed to be their leader, handing her one of the pamphlets. "Would you like to learn more about gnomes?"

Lizzie found herself so surprised she forgot to be anxious. "Of course," she said. "Would you like to come in?" Even before she'd been bathed in the waters of the well in the woods, and thus gained the ability to see the magical, she'd been used to out-of-the-ordinary individuals arriving on the Vicarage doorstep, often the mentally ill, whom she did her best to help. In the past, she'd even sometimes found meeting the unexpected like that to be fun. The most fun had been the time when a Jehovah's Witness had knocked on her door, asking her if she'd heard about God. She'd answered in her clerical collar, and had asked him if this was perhaps the apex of his mission, something he'd been training for over months, that he was going to attempt to actually convert a vicar? He'd seemed merely nonplussed and had quickly continued his prepared speech. She'd ended up pursuing him down the driveway, calling on him not to go so soon, to keep reaching for the stars. The poor guy had just been fulfilling the needs of his belief system, but Lizzie hadn't thought too badly of herself afterwards. She had, after all, been asking him to stay. She wondered now if these gnomes were on some sort of religious mission too.

"Err, no thank you," said their leader. "We don't find your buildings suited to our needs."

"Of course," said Lizzie. "Please, continue."

"That's a better welcome than you lot have given us elsewhere," said the angry-looking gnome to the leader's left. "All of this looking out of the door over our heads and only noticing us when we speak. We're deliberately wearing magic to let you all see us. Don't you lot have small people amongst your own kind?"

"We do. And you're right. Sorry."

"Well," said the angry one, looking slightly disappointed—he'd obviously been spoiling for a fight. "We'll say no more about it."

"Gavin, please," said the leader, "let's not be churlish in the face of the most courteous welcome we've had. And now I've got a good long look at you, Rev-er-end"—he spoke it as carefully as Lizzie might enunciate the title of a faith leader from another tradition—"I understand why. You're one of the Wise Woman's coven."

"I don't call it that," said Lizzie quickly, "but sure."

"I think perhaps the easiest way to do this," said the leader, "is to ask you to read our literature." He gestured toward the pamphlet.

After a few moments of reading, Lizzie found that her anxiety had returned in its entirety.

Zoya Boyko was from Odessa in Ukraine, which had, on and off, been near the front line in the Russian invasion. Every day her social media was full of reports of the places she'd grown up around being destroyed in explosions. She was doomscrolling again as she sat behind the counter of Witches, the magic shop, which was, unfortunately and understandably, thanks to the local supernatural weirdness, possibly now the most well-frequented magic shop in the world. She didn't want to deal with customers who were worried that they were seeing things their cat couldn't. She wanted to go back home and fight. She thought that every day. And yet her daughter, Jas, was doing amazingly in the local school, despite her autism, and there was nobody else to look after her. Zoya's extended family were still in Odessa. So she sent what little money she could afford and found herself full of impotent fury at least a couple of times a week. A particular source of stress was when some TV personality here had some scandal and suddenly that, *that*, was the focus of the national news! When the pool she had learned to swim in had just been destroyed by a cruise missile!

Autumn, her boss here, had listened and listened, and would always listen, and had raised Zoya's wages as far as she could and had told her if she ever did want to go, she would look after Jas and give Zoya a bag of spells to take with her.

But... but... Jas was only ten, and she had difficulty with any adults that weren't Zoya or her teachers or

Louise, the neighbor who was right now babysitting for her as the shop did its Friday evening stocktaking. And her family at home kept telling her no, that she should stay safe here. So did the three other Ukrainian families who'd arrived at the school. They all took care to talk English to each other in the playground, desperate to do everything they could to show gratitude for this precarious sanctuary. Zoya even felt guilty for getting here first, for having arrived as a result of Jas' dad's unworthiness. She had consulted her mother's books, the ones that had first told her about magic, seeking some form of attack, but she had found only mazes. Autumn had said that might have been her mother's idea of protecting the reader from buying a spell for which the price would be too high. Zoya thought Autumn's belief that all magic was undiscovered science was foolish, and yet she had to admit that the town's "Wise Woman" did have a ton of emotional intelligence.

"You would not believe the mess Luke's made of the bedroom," said Autumn, entering from the back of the shop, making notes on her iPad. "He just leaves his clothes everywhere. He's like a T-Rex—if something stops moving he can't see it."

"Oh," said Zoya, closing the scroll of burning buildings on her phone. "That is so awful."

"Not awful," said Autumn. "I mean, still got that newlywed joy going. It's just that . . . sometimes I could make good use of an electric cattle prod."

Zoya wondered distantly if Autumn told Lizzie about all these slight dissatisfactions of her married life. They would be like tiny stabs of hope to Lizzie's heart. Hurts that Lizzie could never acknowledge, even to herself. And following Lizzie's slightly drunken confession one evening about her feelings toward Autumn, Zoya now saw the result of those stabs every time she saw Lizzie, saw that slight weight on the priest's shoulders, without Autumn—for all her emotional intelligence—being at all aware of what she was doing. Zoya felt these two really should have an honest conversation. Because this situation could get extremely sour.

And yet it was very much not her place to interfere.

There was a sudden thumping on the door. Autumn opened it, and in rushed Lizzie, waving a piece of paper. "The gnomes," she said, "are distributing a list of their demands."

"The what now?" said Zoya.

Autumn quickly filled in some gaps in her knowledge of supernatural beings. "They're usually incredibly laid-back. What do they want?"

Lizzie read from the leaflet. "They demand that 'the old promise must be kept,' whatever that means. That 'crude depictions of their bodies and culture' must cease—"

"Do they mean—?"

"Garden gnomes."

"Around here, that's a big ask."

"That's not the worst of it. They want the war memorial changed to 'make it sound true.'"

"Oh," said Zoya. "This sort of thing I understand. This will cause terrible consequences."

Autumn Blunstone took a long, deep breath, held it, let it out again. She had ceased the really quite urgently needed stocktaking at her shop, made tea for her two friends, and had them all sit down at the big table she'd now made the centrepiece of her backroom laboratory/sanctum sanctorum, or whatever it was called in the Marvel movies.

Working with these two was proving to be a lot harder than working with dear old Judith had been, when it really should have been the opposite, given how much help they now had from locals who now, literally, believed in what they were doing. Zoya was understandably distracted a lot of the time, but lately Lizzie, who should have been able to pick up that weight, seemed pretty much out of it too. Autumn still didn't believe in Lizzie's God—who, like those of all the established religions, remained handily invisible to the supernatural senses of those who'd partaken of this town's mystical water—but she respected her best friend's absolute steadfastness and willingness to go the extra mile to care for people. Right now, though, Lizzie would sometimes treat Autumn like they'd just met, sometimes try too hard, sometimes be weirdly angry at her. It was like Lizzie had lost the script for the play they were both in and was proving to be terrible at improv.

"So," she said, "what do we know about gnomes?"

"According to my mother's books," said Zoya, "the Nom is the spirit of a dead farmer, sort of. It's unclear. When one builds a new farm, they might already be there on the land, and they'll help to make things, secretly, in the night, or in the moments when nobody's about. They like to build and they stand in judgment of humans. That is to say they sometimes disapprove of what we have done with a farm or a building."

"That sounds exactly like what's happening now," said Lizzie. "I suppose we haven't heard from them in ages because we haven't pissed them off in ages."

"The Gnommen Ken," said Autumn, "is what they themselves call the nation of gnomes, in the pocket dimension—"

"The other world," corrected Zoya.

Autumn paused for a second, almost pleased that

there was still someone in the room who would object to her science like Judith had. Almost. "Their own land everyone can now access just by walking in the woods."

"I wonder if that's contributed," said Lizzie. "They're used to only meeting humans on their own terms."

"Right," said Autumn, pleased that Lizzie was taking part. "Gnome hermits used to live in human houses if they liked a human family, and could magically remain unseen. That seems to have been a recurring cultural thing for them."

"I wonder why," said Lizzie. "I mean, what does the gnome get out of it? Just a bit of cheese from the fridge after dark?"

"No idea. But these days, around here at least, secrecy like that isn't on the cards, and things have become a bit more concrete and confrontational. The gnome king was a signatory to the peace treaty. You remember, he was at the ceremony."

"Oh yes, he looked great. Exactly like a ... garden gnome. Oh dear."

"That bit of their demands," said Zoya, "I understand. I mean, garden gnomes, from what I've found online, they are a new thing. From the 1930s. Perhaps with the different rates of time passing in the other worlds, and the gnomes' long lifespans, they have only just noticed that they are represented in gardens as these cute little characters."

"And then there are those two other demands," said Lizzie, "about an 'old promise'—"

"I can't find any reference to that anywhere," said Autumn.

"—and about the wording on the war memorial, which is deeply weird. Why do they care about how humans commemorate their wars?"

"Again," said Autumn, "we have no idea. There's nothing in the peace treaty that specifically refers to their needs. I mean, I thought they came along to the ceremony just because they were a race who had a land that bordered ours and so had an interest in the result. If they'd wanted to be treated differently, surely that was the point to mention it?"

"It was a very quickly written treaty," said Zoya, "and I bet the specific needs of the other nations weren't thought of very much during the drafting process."

"A lot of it was written by the elves," said Autumn, "but I understand the other nations were invited to contribute. There have been meetings of the truth and reconciliation commission, which was my idea, and the gnomes haven't even attended."

"Perhaps this is a generational thing," said Zoya. "Passions have ignited *since* the treaty."

"You mean the gnomes are being radicalized?" said Lizzie.

"If you wish to use this word."

"I seem to remember Judith saying something," said Lizzie, "about gnome markings being left on buildings, about gnomes being able to... build in what *you'd* call other dimensions and *you'd* call other worlds. 'Build summat in people's dreams and imaginations if they want to,' that's what she said. It stayed with me because it sounded so odd."

"We definitely don't know enough about them," said Autumn. "Do you reckon they're going to call here?"

"I think they already did," said Zoya, pointing.

Autumn saw that the usual pile of mail spam on the other end of the table included something that was shining in the way which indicated it was not of this world. "Oh bollocks." She pulled out another copy of the leaflet that Lizzie had brought over. "If the shop's shut I have sometimes ignored the doorbell. I'm sorry, I just... sometimes need time to..."

"It's all right," said Zoya. "How about we go talk to the gnome king, see if we can sort this out?"

"I..." Lizzie seemed to have been about to come out with a protest but then stopped herself. "Yes. Absolutely we should." *Oh God, why is she looking so worried about it?*

"You don't have to come. This is a mission for the

Wise Woman and her apprentice, and it'll just be a lot of talking."

"Right." Lizzie nodded. "Okay. Thanks. Tell me how it goes. I'll be off. Parish stuff to do. Good luck." And without quite making eye contact, she bustled out of the room.

Autumn wanted to call out to her, but something about the way Lizzie was shutting her out right now seemed so final, so resolute... Autumn heard the shop door close behind her before she could start to say anything. She looked to Zoya. "What is going on with her right now?"

Zoya's expression was a blank. "No idea at all."

2

"HI, I'M ROBIN DANIELS of the *Unworldly* podcast, and here I am with my brave as always sound engineer Logan—he's raising an eyebrow at that—in the marketplace of the quaint little Cotswolds market town of Lychford. I say 'quaint,' but you may have heard... stories... about this place. Stories that make the calm, placid façade of this town on a summer afternoon, a scene with the odd pensioner strolling by, people walking their dogs... seem like just that: a façade. Stories that, if they're true... can't easily be explained by science. We're here to see if we can discover what lies beneath the surface of Lychford. I'm Robin Daniels, and this... is *Unworldly*."

(Cue spooky theme music.)

"So, one of the oddest things about a place the name of which has now come to mean, for some people, the supernatural... it's got a magic shop. That is to say, it has Witches, a place that sells crystal balls, herbs, occult books, paraphernalia. I'm looking at Autumn Blunstone, a tall woman in her thirties, with colorful ribbons in her hair, and she's wearing the most amazing... costume with colors that don't seem to really fit with each... I'm not sure what that *is* she's got on, honestly—"

"It's what I found on the bedroom floor this morning. Is this going to be about my style choices?"

"Okay, mark a possible edit here. I always describe who we're talking to—"

"I'm very busy. We're preparing for—"

"A trip into the woods to forage for herbs."

"This new voice is Zoya Boyko, a short, strong-looking woman in her late twenties, with a sidecut and pierced ears but no earrings—"

"There is no story there. I have a child. Why do you mention this?"

"Possible edit here."

"Listen, sorry, I'm the owner here, why are you in here?"

"I'm here to ask, you both live in this town, perhaps you provide mystical protection to those who feel threatened by the forces many say have been unleashed in this place. Have you ever experienced anything... otherworldly?"

"We're on audio, right? Do you want me to describe my gesture?"

"Not on Radio 4, no."

"We provide metaphorical comforts and meditative

aid. I believe in science, not magic, in the rational. I've heard your show. You always bring in sceptics, but you weight the scales against them and you never say 'what if our subject this week is just making it up?'"

"So... one last question. Why are you both looking over my shoulder as if there's something behind me?"

"Autumn, allow me to take this: because you have a little something on your shirt there, let me just... oh, there, see? It is gone. As you should be."

"I'm thinking perhaps we should move on."

"Good idea. Let me describe to you the location of the door."

"We're here outside the Station Inn, one of the favorite local watering holes, chatting to the owner, Owen Trafalgar, a smart middle-aged man in a waistcoat with a Vandyke beard and a twinkle in his eye—"

"Oh, very nice to hear about the twinkle. We're a local pub, but we also very much welcome tourists. And cyclists. We can be found on social media—"

"It's a modern, vibrant social centre for this town... but in this town you must hear... stories."

"We absolutely do hear stories, yes. That's just one of the pleasures of drinking in our beer garden here—"

"Stories of the weird events that have befallen the locals in this town—"

"Not really, no. All sorts of stories. But I don't think I've ever heard anything about elves or demons or ghosts or anything like that."

"Really?"

"Not . . . that I recall."

"One thing we do on our podcast, we make a point of believing everyone we talk to."

"Great. Good policy."

"I don't think there's much here we can use, though."

"Oh well."

"So, here's a question: Why do you keep looking over my shoulder as if there's something behind me?"

"I need to visit the optician. It's a squint."

"Is that really what you were doing? Is the pub itself perhaps . . . haunted?"

"No, absolutely not. People can come here and enjoy our guest rooms, like you yourself are doing, Robin, without worrying about that. We are the least haunted pub in Britain."

"The least haunted? How can you be the least haunted?"

"Because we have zero ghosts."

"Aren't there lots of pubs that have zero ghosts?"

"Then it's a tie. We're in a tie for the least haunted

pub in Britain. But, you know, if we could have minus one ghosts, we would."

"We're at the imposing doors of St. Martin's, the historic parish church of Lychford, and, oh, come on, Logan, coming out of those doors is the local vicar. Hello, Reverend—"

"Oh, err, Lizzie, hello."

"Are you okay with being on Radio 4?"

"I . . . yes, I suppose. I mean, there's no reason why I wouldn't be, is there?"

"And look, here, again, immediately, why are you looking over my shoulder?"

"There was an interesting pigeon. Just there. I do . . . I can't remember what it's called now, that thing I do, about people liking birds?"

"You seem a little anxious, Reverend."

"I am, yes, thank you for noticing."

"Is it perhaps because you're responsible for the spiritual welfare of the people of this town? Because if they feel vulnerable about the impossible, the supernatural, it's down to you to make them feel better, isn't it?"

"I . . . yes. Now you put it like that . . . I'm going to have to sit down, excuse me."

"Are you sure you're okay with carrying on?"

"Yes. Yes. Is this going to go out around the same time as *The Archers*?"

"We're rather more for the late-night crowd."

"Oh. Well, I'm often busy then. I mean, asleep. I'm asleep. Because of my enormous spiritual burden. Which I deal with in the daytime."

"Have you ever had an encounter with something... difficult to explain?"

"There are some entries to our 'make a cake depicting the church' contest that are very difficult to explain."

"Reverend, are you... being evasive?"

"I'm doing the best I can in difficult circumstances, wouldn't you say? That's what I'd say. And that's all I'm going to say. Oh look, another pigeon."

"We're taking a break in one of the locals' favorite coffee houses. It's called 7a, after the address, it's on the High Street and it's run by an absolutely everyday couple, Mr. and Mrs. Morris. Over there, which is why I'm keeping my voice down, there's what looked, when we came in, like a rather fractious meeting of what I take to be the town council. But since it's become clear what we're doing here, they've stopped talking and are just glaring at each other. Ah, here comes Mrs. Morris now, in her apron, with long brown hair and an engaged, happy look on her face."

"Oh, thank you, I try!"

"It's a bit quiet in here now, isn't it?"

"No. For the audience at home, it's packed. With people."

"But they're ... being a bit quiet. And there it is again: what is it you're looking at over my shoulder?"

"I was just thinking it's a lovely day outside. You'd be happier in the garden, probably."

"One of the council is getting up, the one I believe is called Jim, an elderly man with some extraordinary facial hair, and he's heading for the door. Excuse me, Jim—"

"I'm not going to be on your so-called podcast. I'm against them. Now if you'll get out of my way—"

"We're not in your way, Jim."

"I weren't talking to you. Goodbye!"

"Did you hear that? If we needed encouragement, if we needed a reason to think we're not here on a fool's errand... well, bloody hell, Jim. You've given us what we need to keep going. Oh, Logan, did you get that? Was that a... mysterious groaning sound? You're listening to the *Unworldly* podcast, I'm Robin Daniels. And we're here in Lychford. Wondering."

(Cue spooky theme music.)

Autumn had quickly locked up the shop, and, with a carpet bag of magical resources over her shoulder, headed out toward the river, Zoya following. Over the bridge and onto the footpaths to get into the woods, and from there it was just a hike to get across the borders into any of the neighboring magical lands. Many of them had now put in place gentle magical discouragements to nudge wandering humans toward deciding that the opposite direction looked to have more promising picnic sites. The terms of the treaty allowed for this. What was important was that any inhabitant of the Many Worlds could, if they had made a conscious decision to cross a border, achieve that aim.

As they walked, Autumn checked her texts and immediately had to reply to three in a row from Luke. He was really very good about trusting her in crisis situations, but he needed to know where she was.

```
Just keep me in mind, over here
at the college, finishing up some
summer paperwork. I'll be back home
for dinner. Will make you something:
freezer or fridge?
```

>   Frudge. Frudge. Fridge.

You okay?

>   Autocorrect. Not Brian damage.

You on the move? Heading for Gnomeland?

>   Yep. Love you.

Love you. Frudge. Lx.

Autumn pocketed the phone. "Now we've got to be back tonight or he'll worry."

"So..." Zoya seemed to be on the verge of asking something huge, but finally sighed and instead smiled brightly. "How are you two doing?"

"Still in the Just Married phase. Fun. Finding out about each other."

"I do not want to know the details."

"Not like that. And yeah, like that. But also learning all each other's habits, accommodating each other."

"What you said about him leaving the bedroom messy made me wonder—"

"*That* makes you wonder? Wow, do you and Lizzie

both think I can't deal with being married?"

"So Lizzie asked too?"

"Yeah. Who's the Wise Woman here, okay? Mind you, he does like that podcast Robin Daniels does, which drives me mental, which is maybe why I reacted so much to him asking us questions. He's probably a decent bloke—did you notice how he described me without mentioning my skin color? He didn't deserve me blowing up at him, and he also doesn't deserve being followed around by that furious-looking gnome who's giving him the silent treatment."

"He realized we could all see something behind him."

"Yeah. As to why the gnomes are doing that, well, add that to the list of questions we have for their king."

They walked for a while through the forest, beautiful in the late afternoon sunlight, and crossed the border into the Land of the Gnomes without any visible marker, though Autumn felt it in the same part of her head where she stored, it turned out, smell memories of baked potatoes. And so to move from human land to otherwise was, for her, to move from summer into the season she was named for. The associations went alongside the magic, the poetry of both interlacing in her mind like entwined strands of DNA. It always amazed her how little Judith had talked about these enhanced senses, the business of the Wise Woman. Then again, she'd had so few people to talk to before Autumn and Lizzie had come along. What Judith had had to do in her role had alienated her from those she defended. And Autumn thought then of Lizzie.

But before she could resolve how different those situations were, they came upon the outskirts of a gnome town, a complex of earthen mounds with stone buildings further on, all interlaced with and supported by the trees.

Autumn could immediately feel the sentries in the long grass around them. She raised a hand. "Wise Woman visiting," she said. "Under the terms of the treaty."

"Take us to your leader," said Zoya.

The gnome king was about half a metre tall, and wore a golden, ceremonial version of the work apron and tool belt she'd seen on a lot of gnomes; plus, of course, more facial hair than seemed feasible. His little blue eyes peered from a mass of it like he was a particularly perplexed beagle. His name, oddly to Autumn's ears, was Greg. That was bound to happen from time to time, though. The chosen names of other races would sometimes seem very like human ones. "Greetings, Wise Woman," he said, in what was, again surprisingly, something very like a Gloucestershire accent. "These are my advisors, Malcolm and Stu."

"Oh," said Autumn.

"What?" said the king. "Is summat wrong?"

"Not at all, Your Grace," said Autumn, executing the proper bow in front of the three ancient gnomes as Zoya did the same beside her. "This is my apprentice."

"Oh ah," said King Greg, looking her up and down. "Well, this is Tracey, the gnomette."

A female gnome, in the same sort of ceremonial gear, but with an enormous pile of blonde hair, stepped forward. "Gnomette?" said Zoya.

"I," said Tracey, "am the only woman gnome of this generation."

"Oh," said Autumn again. "And . . . how's that working out for you?"

"Great," said Tracey, a contented little smile on her face.

They retired to the interior of a barrow, which turned out to be an ornate council chamber. Autumn and Zoya were able to enter through big ceremonial doors, but once inside an antechamber they found themselves suddenly shrinking. Zoya cried out, but Autumn called to her to just go with it.

They ended up sitting around an enormous and beautiful stone table, on little wooden seats that looked like toadstools. Autumn made a mental note not to mention that. She very much believed in taking other cultures on their own terms, but sometimes actually doing that was pretty damn difficult.

"I expected your own king to come along," said King Greg. "Will he be joining us?"

"He's a bit busy," said Autumn. "And of course he doesn't represent all humans."

"Ah, so I recall. Bloody odd setup you got there. But don't think that lets you off the hook for yet another bloody insult. Before you ask your questions, and I think I know what they're going to be, what's up with all this bad weather of yours? Since the borders came down, there's been too much sunshine and too much rain and too much existential doom flooding into the Many Worlds."

Autumn tried her best to explain climate change. She felt it acutely with her magical senses, a slow chaotic decay under everything, particularly when there was one of the larger and scarier storms they seemed to be getting so many more of in the Cotswolds. Still, it didn't seem to get to her as much as it got to Lizzie, maybe because they'd prevented the actual end of the world on several previous occasions. In the end the king just told her to clean up her own mess, and Autumn could only say she'd do her best. "As you realized, Your Grace," she continued, "I'm here about your people in Lychford right now, and the nature of your demands."

The king puffed out his cheeks. "The old promise must be kept. The memorial to your war must be made to sound true."

"Yes, if you could please explain—"

"It's beneath us to explain those, love. Ours to declare, yours to know. Because you really bloody should. But because it pleases me, let me tell you what the other one is all about."

"Yes, the one concerning 'crude depictions of your culture.'"

"Since that last big war of yours when things were blowing up on your soil on a regular basis, you lot have been putting small statues of my people in your gardens. What's that about?"

"I . . . don't actually know," said Autumn.

"Me neither," said Zoya, "but we did it in Odessa too."

"When that began it was just insulting. Our lot and your lot, we go back a long way. Where do you think your accent comes from? And our culture is easily swayed by whatever's going on in yours, running parallel to yours on a magical basis, which is frankly bloody annoying. But yours gains from ours, too, in secret ways, under ancient rules known only to the select few. So we'd expect a bit more respect. But no. And lately it's got worse: little statues making rude gestures, or doing rude things—"

"Or dressed like characters from *Star Trek*," said Autumn, thinking about a particular fixture in the Vicarage garden.

"So, take that as the only extra clarity you'll be getting today. Keep the old promise. Make the memorial sound true, but above all else, get rid of those bloody 'garden gnomes.'"

"Or—?" said Zoya.

"Or," said the gnome king, "we'll make some garden ornaments of our own."

Lizzie really did not like the feeling of being stared at in horror by everyone present at a full Extraordinary General Meeting of Lychford Town Council. She got the feeling that these days pretty much all their meetings must be Extraordinary, and this one could more accurately be described as Incredible.

"That's exactly what your ... colleagues in the ...

Land of the ... the ..."

"Gnomes," said Lizzie, helping along Carrie Anne Christopher's sentence. She could see Loz, the town clerk, take a moment before tapping in the words.

"That's what they reported?"

Lizzie pointed to her phone. "You can read the texts if you like. Now, you usually trust the three of us about stuff like this. Autumn would like to go ahead and start negotiating, offer to do something about the garden gnomes right away and use that bargaining chip to dig into what the king means by these other two—"

"Absolutely not," said Jim, whom Lizzie knew only from having to stand behind him in the chip shop when he was having a row about portion sizes. To her surprise, he now rose to his feet and grasped his lapels, his eyebrow hairs bristling. "Do you think you can come here and have us rubber-stamp such ridiculousness, Reverend?"

"I *was* rather hoping—"

"The war memorial in the marketplace commemorates the fallen of this town and dates back to the First World War! Do not you yourself conduct a service there every Remembrance Sunday? Do these local heroes mean nothing to you? Do their families, members of whom still live in this town, mean nothing?"

"I ... I can see that ..." Lizzie felt like the room was

physically closing in on her. She could feel a tension down one side of her neck and into her shoulder. What was *wrong* with her? Addressing an audience wasn't some phobia of hers, she did it every week.

"I say no," Jim continued, oblivious, "to changing the words on something our people created, in our town, just because they might offend a tiny minority of . . . so-called gnomes! Everyone is taking offense at everything these days, now including, it seems, people who aren't even people! We should be proud of our past. We should defend it. We have gnomes in our streets, we have so-called podcasters in our streets, we have Radio 4! The ears of the world are upon us! I do not recognize any so-called promises this town might have made to these non-people people, and I for one will not be taking a single gnome out of my garden! If they want my gnomes, these so-called gnomes can come and try it!"

To Lizzie's horror, there was a small smattering of applause.

Jim looked around, quite surprised at this unusual response, but worryingly pleased by it. Sunil had an angry look on his face and was shaking his head, but Jackie Parker was cautiously nodding, and Matt Coomby, whom Lizzie might have expected to take a stand against bigotry, was looking like he had just tasted a particularly complicated wine and was carefully formulating a review.

"Well," he began, "both sides—"

"Listen." Lizzie found herself interrupting, aware of the desperation in her voice. "We can fix this. It's our job to fix this. Just let us quietly do our thing and—"

"No," said Jim, slamming his palm on the meeting table. "You brought this to us for our approval, Reverend. So we are going to have a vote."

Lizzie looked to Dave, who had an oddly awkward expression on his face. "Yeah," he said. "I can see how this is going to go. Carrie, can we move to a vote please? Then I'll go and tell the gnomes."

"What?!" said Lizzie. "No—"

"There are things about the magic in this town, Reverend," said Dave, quite gently, "that even dear old Judith never knew."

Lizzie found herself ushered out, and, feeling more lost than she ever had, sat down in the empty hallway outside the chamber. What was all that about? The other councillors didn't seem to know. They were just caught up in this . . . horrifying spiral into . . .

Lizzie found that, before she could text Autumn to tell her what was happening here, she had to practice her deep breathing exercises for several minutes.

Loz had her own views about what had happened that evening in the council chamber, but she knew her own duty was to never reveal what those views were. She had, however, mainly because she was curious, volunteered to go with Dave as he headed down to the little bridge over the river in the gathering gloom of a summer's night.

There were other circumstances in which she would have preferred to have been walking here with him on such a night. She sometimes thought that the wonders of actual magic deflected attention from the everyday magic formed by the low light on the river, the wind in the trees, and the calling of the birds as they found their homes. That magic was now just a metaphor, and dangerous magic, the magic of sudden change rather than the magic of very slow change, was concrete. But such thoughts weren't helpful right now. Dave had a grim look on his hard, yet somehow also caring, features. He was wearing his chain of office and had thrown on a jacket. Lizzie, on hearing the result of the vote, had had to be actually physically restrained from coming with them. "Are you sure this is a good idea?" she said.

"No," said Dave, "but it's got to be done."

"But I don't get it. Why you this time? Why not the Wise Woman and the vicar?"

He paused for a moment before visibly deciding to tell her. "Because I'm one of the reasons they're here.

The gnomes. They've been following me around, saying stuff—"

"They've been *talking* to you? What about?"

He shook his head. "I think I know what one of their demands is about. Let's just say . . . we have a history."

3

LOZ FOLLOWED DAVE to the part of the forest where numerous rough signs had been put up—some with the town council's permission, some without—warning walkers that from this point their maps weren't going to be much use, that from here on there was actually a lot more forest than they might have been expecting, that children shouldn't be allowed here unsupervised, and that honestly their best course of action would be to get on home. Dave had refused to answer any of her many questions. This mystery about how he knew so much that previously Loz had thought was the domain of the Wise Woman didn't make her feel alienated from him; it just increased the sense of Dave being quite the meaningful individual. Perhaps some form of invitation might be in order, to join her and a group of her mates down the pub, or no, bolder than that: a request to go to the first night of the Women's Institute's over-seventies production of *Cabaret*. Such thoughts kept Loz's mind off the surroundings as they entered the kind of area where she found herself wary of the shadows and the odd sounds of the birds. Finally, Dave stopped. "Yeah," he said, "there it is."

All Loz could see was the remains of an old dry-stone wall. Or rather two of them, in parallel, both running for about two metres, with a metre's gap in between. Dave walked carefully between the walls, took the piece of paper from his pocket that contained the agreed-upon Council message to the gnomes, picked up a stone from the ground, and, after a moment's consideration, carefully placed it on one of the walls.

Something around them, perhaps the light, perhaps something more important like gravity, changed. Loz found herself in a moment of dreaming. Standing beside the wall, looking up at Dave, stood a gnome. It looked at the single stone Dave had added and blew out a long breath in a dismissive fashion. Sighing, it held out its hand.

Dave offered it the piece of paper. It took it, looked again at him with what seemed like great disappointment, and vanished.

"There," said Dave. "Now they know. God help us."

Zoya and Autumn had spent a timeless time in the gnome stronghold, waiting for a reply to Autumn's last text to Lizzie. They had been allowed to leave the barrow, grow in size once more, and wander through the small streets. Zoya had felt, as she'd stepped carefully over markets and thoroughfares, rather like some enormous cinematic monster that was about to flatten Tokyo. She was trying hard to be diplomatic, but that was very difficult when scratching your leg with your foot might result in the destruction of someone's house. She and Autumn finally settled under a tree that seemed free of all building work. "Time seems to flow at a different rate here," she said.

Autumn glanced at her phone. "No," she said, "it's just a bit dull."

Zoya could feel the nervousness of her mentor, even if she was trying not to show it. "Why do you think it is taking so long for the Lychford Town Council to decide on this?"

"I don't know if it is. I think it might be Lizzie being... I don't know. She just seems scared all the time lately. I'm worried about her. And I'm worried about her dropping the ball. When 'the ball' might be, I don't know, the universe."

Zoya pursed her lips. "Do you think, perhaps, something is troubling her?"

"Well, yeah, but she won't tell me what. And that's so weird. Me and her, we're like that." Autumn crossed her fingers. "Or I thought we were."

Zoya pointed at the fingers. "What *is* that?"

"Oh, isn't this a thing in Ukraine? It means great friends, best buddies."

"Yeah," sighed Zoya. "That is what I thought." She might have been about to tentatively start to suggest what the nature of Lizzie's discomfort might be, but at that moment there came a small sound of hammers on stone, which was presumably the gnome equivalent of a fanfare, and from the barrow marched King Greg, Tracey the gnomette, and several more of those who'd been present at the conference. And they weren't looking happy.

"Hoi," called the king. "You two. Lend us yer lugholes. We've heard word from your stronghold."

"But—" Autumn began, glancing again at her phone.

"Through the old channels," said the king. "The ways known only to us and those like us."

"What ways do you know that I don't?" said Autumn, looking profoundly shocked.

"Never mind that, luv, you're missing the point here. Your lot aren't having it. Nada. Our completely reasonable demands were thrown back in our faces. There's even language in here about us taking those obscene garden statues of theirs out of their cold, dead hands. Well, so bloody be it. Steps are going to have to be taken. Now, I'm going to stand by the letter of the treaty. You two get safe passage out of here. But you'd best scarper, because I can order my guards not to hurt you, but I can't speak for the gnome in the street, so to speak, and a lot of my folk are what you might call well and truly radicalized."

"No," said Autumn. "Please, listen, we need to stay and talk about this—"

"No more bloody chat!" bellowed Tracey. And with that she grabbed a pebble off the ground and threw it.

It bounced off Zoya's ankle. "Ow," she said.

"Tracey," sighed the king, "knock it off, girl. I made a promise."

"All right, all right," said the gnomette. "I'll respect how it has to be. For now. For here. But after that I'll be getting my bottom-kicking boots out of the cupboard. These two should spread the word to their people. The time for a nice cosy chat is over. They had every chance to do that. Now is the time for fire and blood." She marched up to Autumn and poked her in the knee. "This evening," she declared, "will come a reckoning. This evening you should fear midnight. This evening Lychford will face the Night of the Gnomes."

Lizzie was used to walking anxiously now—from the extra breath it took from her, to the extra weight it put in her shoulders and chest—but as the summer sun descended in the sky that evening, she felt the anxiety more than ever. She said a prayer for herself under her breath, but she'd been praying about this for so long now, and every time she did she felt decadent, because there was so much else in the world that was more important. She'd gone out with the thought in her mind that she would find out what was taking Autumn and Zoya so long, that she would head up toward the woods and see if she could meet them coming back, because why had their texts stopped so suddenly? But having got across the river and halfway up to the woods with no sign of them, it had suddenly felt more urgent for her to go back into town.

Was this her magical senses doing what they should? Or was it just her anxiety doing what it did, dragging her first one way, then another? Just the thought of patrolling the town forced her mind to frantically pace like an animal in a zoo. She put her head into the pubs, said a breathless hello to the early drinkers outside. She waved to the staff of the coffee places as they brought chairs in and locked up. She kept feeling like she would see Autumn at any moment.

Oh God, what if she'd lost her? Without having said—but what could she have said? What on earth would ever be useful, would ever make a difference?

Besides, that was a stupid thought. Just because her

texts had stopped. The gnomes might well know of the town's reaction by now, but that was more likely to have resulted in some sort of magical communications blackout than the previously friendly creatures actually harming—

Lizzie stopped short as her eyes insisted to her brain that what they were seeing was more important than her fevered imaginings right now. She had been marching along one of the more middle-class terraced streets; not quite the sort of place where there were electric gates and driveways, but still a series of houses with precisely maintained gardens at the front.

In the one she'd stopped in front of, between the flowerbeds, something was on fire.

It was the bottom half of a garden gnome. The top of it had vanished, and the base was blazing like a torch. That was the sort of impossible that Lizzie had got used to over the last few years, but to see such violence in a country garden was still somehow shocking, especially since the fire was big enough to catch light to a nearby fence, to spread—! She ran up the garden path to the house and rang the doorbell.

Which was when she saw what had been scrawled on the window in the sort of rough, tottering hand that one might get if the scrawler was a small person standing on the shoulders of other small people.

End Gnomesploitation Now! it said. And the exclamation mark zipped off to the right as if the writer had fallen sideways.

The door opened, revealing Edith Plummery, in her eighties and a member of Lizzie's congregation, the sort of old lady who never said hello to her but who was out of the church door in her best shoes at high speed as the last organ note sounded. "Reverend?!" she said, her voice quavering, as if the sight of a cleric in her garden meant that the end times were approaching. Actually, thought Lizzie, given that the end times had genuinely been approaching pretty recently and Lizzie had been rather visibly active in stopping them, maybe that wasn't such an extreme reaction.

"Edith," she said, "your gnome is on fire."

Edith slowly stepped outside and gazed in horror, but then her gaze lifted to take in the whole street. "Oh dear," she said. "It's not the only one."

Lizzie looked. And sure enough, in several gardens there were similar plumes of smoke. Lizzie managed not to swear. "We need to call—" she began, grabbing her phone, but then she realized—the local fire station was outside the area that had been affected by the magical rain. The firefighters might be in danger from angry gnomes and wouldn't be able to see what was attacking them. "Bucket chain!" she called. "Come on!" And she rushed inside Edith's house to find some sort of bucket.

Ten minutes later, everyone in the street who'd got home that evening was out with a vessel carrying water. After she'd helped extinguish Edith's gnome, Lizzie felt able to go down the street and assess the damage. Not a gnome remained intact. There were several messages scrawled on walls and windows, and in one instance on a very downcast-looking beagle. They ranged from the reasonably literate *Personhood not Ornamentation!* to the specific *That Looked like my Grandad and you'd Let Moss Grow on Him!* to full-on sweary rudeness about humans that Lizzie tried to wash off before anyone saw.

But water wouldn't shift these words.

The gnomes seemed to have learned English specifically in order to do this. Or perhaps the magical sight everyone had was doing the translating.

If the gnomes had done this here, what had they done elsewhere?

Oh no—the war memorial!

Lizzie broke into a run, as best she could, and the exertion actually made the anxiety feel a bit better. On the wall of the coffee shop at the corner of the marketplace there had been painted—one could hardly say "daubed"—a tiny fist in a white glove that was... a bit cartoony. Oh dear, had that been a racist thought on her part? If only Lizzie could have actually encountered any of the gnomes doing this, she might have been able to start some sort of parlay with them, bypass this ridiculous reply the council had made—but she hadn't seen any sign of them. It seemed that, when they wanted to, the gnomes could pass invisibly through the world of humans—even humans that could see magical beings.

Lizzie ran on into the marketplace itself and found, as well as a growing number of worried and frightened locals—some of whom had come out from the Boar and were clutching pints—there was the war memorial, still intact, and with nothing new written on it.

What did that mean?

She suddenly realized something. She raced back to the vicarage. She stopped at the gate as she saw, in the flowerbeds by the door, the remains of three of her own gnomes blazing. There was a gnome in a Starfleet captain's shirt, his head half gone, his expression now permanently startled. There was another in a science officer's shirt, stoic but headless. And there was a gnome in a red shirt, lying on his front, his hair on fire.

Lizzie felt ridiculously sad to see them. "My... my husband gave me those," she said out loud, in case the culprits were still around. "He died a few years ago. We had no idea you existed then. We thought all this was . . . harmless."

There was no reply.

From toward the marketplace there came a sudden, enormous concussion, like thunder. Flames burst above the tree line. A building on the High Street must be on fire.

Lizzie grabbed the phone from her pocket and urgently started hitting nines. She hated that she felt it, but there was anger in her heart now. So, okay, the fire brigade could deal with this one. Even though it might put them in danger. And once they had, she was going to do something about finding the gnomes responsible.

Loz and Dave had returned to their town to find parts of it literally on fire. The main conflagration turned out to be the old Meredith house, which was one of a couple of ruins awaiting attention from builders, and while Dave was doing his best to calm people down, the fire brigade arrived from halfway to Minton Maisey and started hosing. It didn't look like the blaze was going to spread to any other properties.

Loz asked after the Wise Woman and her lot and were told the vicar had retreated into the Vicarage and the other two were nowhere to be seen. Loz didn't like the gathering tone of panic and anger in the voices of the locals, but she couldn't help but share in some of it. "I mean, you know them, right?" she said to Dave when she had a moment to get him away from the crowds. "Why are they doing this to us?"

"They're doing it carefully," said Dave, sounding exasperated. "That house fire was set so it wouldn't spread, and none of these garden fires will either. They're builders like me. If we could only find some of them and talk one to one—"

"Too late for that," said a voice from behind them. Loz turned to see Jim, at the head of . . . an actual mob with . . . no they weren't actual flaming torches, just electric ones. He was looking angrier than she'd ever seen him, and that was saying a lot.

"Go home, Jim," said Dave.

"You hear that?" Jim turned to his audience. "We're being attacked by so-called magical monsters, and our mayor says we should just quietly go home!" He turned back to them and pointed in Dave's face. "What, you want us to sit quietly while our homes burn down around us?"

For a moment, Loz feared for Jim's safety, but when Dave spoke it was quiet. "This is as far as they'll go. Unless we escalate. What are you planning to do, Jim?"

"I don't know how you know what the enemy are planning. There's going to be an inquiry after this, and I'm going to make sure you and your lot, the people who are close to all this so-called magic, are held responsible. These brave people and I are going to patrol the town, and if we find any of these so-called gnomes, we're going to do to them what they did to us."

"Double!" called a voice from the back.

"You're going to burn small effigies of humans, twice?" said Loz. But nobody in the crowd was listening to her. As she watched, Jim led the mob off down the street, their torches flickering into every crevice in search of the enemy. "They can't do any harm if they can't find them," she said to Dave, but it felt more like she was saying it to herself. "Can they?"

Autumn and Zoya had run pretty much all the way back from the Land of the Gnomes to Lychford. At least most of it had been downhill. But this had been running like Autumn had only rarely experienced it, running with the fear of ambush from all around them. The king of the gnomes had been as good as his word in terms of them not being attacked right there and then, but movements in the foliage and the trees in the low light, broken only by the lights of town ahead, had convinced both of them that they were being at least watched and possibly pursued.

So it was with shaking hands that Autumn found the keys to the shop in her pocket and unlocked the store.

"There is fire," said Zoya, breathing less hard than Autumn was. "They've set on fire a building."

And sure enough, there it was, up in the main part of town, glimpsed between the other houses. "Okay," said Autumn, "we need to stop this now. We need to get Lizzie, work together, build a magical working of some kind to create a barrier against the gnomes."

"We're putting up a barrier again? After they just came down?" Zoya didn't sound entirely displeased at the idea, but the expression on her face was that of a minion who just wanted a little clarification from her supervillain boss.

"Which would break the agreement, and that would let the actual powers of evil do all manner of things, so no, new plan, not going to do that, thank you for the input." Autumn shoved open the door and hustled Zoya inside. She hit the lights, then hit the Lizzie button on her phone. "We are just going to have to find something anti-gnome that's not . . . anti-gnome. Come on, Lizzie, if this goes to voicemail—"

It didn't go to voicemail. Instead there was Lizzie's

voice, sounding like she'd also just been sprinting. "Yes?"

Autumn didn't know why, but there was something in that voice that made her feel the need to identify herself. "Lizzie, it's Autumn. Where are you? Can you get to the shop? We need the three of us to work together and come up with some way to—"

"I can't."

"Lizzie, I don't know what's been going on with you lately, and that's on me, I haven't caught up with you, but I really need you here now because—"

"I can't because they're here."

"What?"

"They're in the garden. I came in to make sure everything was okay, and... they've surrounded me. Every time I try to leave... I tried the door, I tried to go out the window... they're firing these little arrows at me. And one of them hit me, and I don't know if it's done something to me—"

"Okay, we're coming to you."

"Autumn, no, people's houses are burning—"

Autumn hated it and loved it when Lizzie got all self-sacrificing. But there was a note in her friend's voice that she really didn't like the sound of, something on the verge of complete collapse that seemed utterly unlike the brave woman she knew. "We help you first. Then you help others. We're coming to get you."

"Hi, I'm Robin Daniels of the *Unworldly* podcast, and my sound engineer Logan and I... we're still in the quaint little Cotswolds market town of Lychford. It's night. It's all kicking off here. There's a building actually on fire. There are smaller fires everywhere. There are crowds in the streets. We're on our feet, recording on the run, we're just trying to work out what's going on. You can hear that I'm breathing hard. I'm Robin Daniels, and this... is *Unworldly*."

(Cue spooky theme music.)

"What the hell? What the hell is *that*? Was there something in those bushes? Logan, did you see it? He's shaking his head. I... we... we should pause here. Let's just catch our breath on this corner. I feel like I'm becoming part of what I'm reporting on. But... I'm not sure how to retain a distance when we don't know what's going on. The people on the street here... they seem extremely scared, but equally, they're... excuse me, ma'am, can you tell us what's going on? Okay, wait a second, thank you for stopping, could you first identify yourself for the recording, please?"

"I'm Loz Watson, the town clerk."

"So, we're watching as a local fire crew attempt to contain a fire, and we've seen smaller fires in various gardens. What's this all about?"

"It's . . . a local festival. The Lychford Fire Festival. And it's got a bit out of hand. Which it doesn't usually do. Because it's very safe. Despite being all about fire."

"Curious. So what does this festival involve?"

"People light fires and carry them about in a parade. That's what Jim and that lot over there are doing. You see they're picking some logs from one of the garden fires, and they'll be . . . oh God, using them as torches?"

"And you would be, sir?"

"Dave Awlish, the mayor."

"So you would know."

"Not how it usually goes, but sure."

"What exactly are they celebrating?"

"Well . . . night not being very good and we want day back, and so fire is a bit like the day, and . . ."

"Interesting. It seems like a very rough sort of folk belief. There's nothing about it, for example, on the town's website."

"Well, we only just started it this year."

"But Loz here referred to previous iterations. You said it usually didn't get out of hand."

"Ah. Those were practices."

"Practices?"

"You've heard the expression 'ritual practice'? Well, we had some, and this was that."

"Yeah, we gave it two or three goes in previous years before this year we—"

"—really went for it! And wow, we really should have practiced more. Because, whoosh, building on fire. Note taken. Seriously, lesson learned."

"Yep. Back to the drawing board."

"I . . . think I'd better leave you two to it. I'm going to go and have a word with Jim, whom we met earlier in the coffee shop."

"Don't feel you have to!"

"And we've moved on from them now. I must say, this isn't an expression I like using on *Unworldly*, but . . . I didn't believe a word of that. Did you, Logan? No, Logan's shaking his head. Okay, we've caught up with Jim and his group here, who are marching pretty determinedly away from the main street. Jim, where are you going?"

"We're just out for a stroll. Oh, did your mic pick up what Stu over there just said?"

"It sounded like he was yelling about burning something."

"No, we're not burning anything. Or anybody."

"Why is that house on fire?"

"That was nothing to do with us. This is a peaceful demonstration."

"A demonstration? We were told it was a festival."

"We're demonstrating that we can hold a festival. Wait a sec. All right, Norman, you take your lads down Norwood Walk; Sheila, round the back of old Benson's house and down the Lanes."

"We're watching as the group splits in two, both with at least one flaming torch. Jim, is what you call a demonstration here actually . . . a mob with flaming torches?"

"I resent the implication we're a so-called mob. We're concerned citizens, that's all."

"What is there to be concerned about? Oh. Jim's now holding up a hand in my face as if we've got a camera. Jim, we're recording audio. Now he's walking away, shaking his head. Though some of his group, they're clearly . . . you can hear it now . . . they're shouting something about burning . . . is that 'homes'? Bloody hell, whose homes are they going to burn next? Over there, I can see another member of the town council. Excuse me, sir, could you tell us your name, please?"

"Sunil Mehra. I was hoping to meet you, Robin. Big fan."

"Oh, are you? Always nice to hear. But right now, could you tell us what's going on here?"

"Well, I think this is an awful demonstration."

"So it is a demonstration?"

"I mean a demonstration of human nature. It's not what Judith would have done."

"Judith being—?"

"That's not important now. Nobody here is telling you the truth, Robin. Instead, they're letting their passions get the better of them. And look at it. It's like *Lord of the Rings* out there."

"You mean *Lord of the Flies*."

"I know what I mean. Follow me, if you'd be so kind."

"Okay, so we're heading after Sunil, down the street toward—"

"—an excellent Indian restaurant, the Curry Master, with a consistent five-star rating on Tripadvisor, and many favorable comments. But it's what's in the back garden that should interest you. Come on through. Don't let the truly mouthwatering scents of our unique combinations of spices distract you. Out here ... okay, it's still happening. What do you see out here?"

"Oh my God. I see ... Logan, get the boom mic out here into the back garden. We're in a small, fenced-off garden, with neatly tended flowerbeds and herbs, except I should say it's formerly neatly tended, because I'm watching as ... is that a garden gnome? It's being thrown around by some sort of ... I can't see anything doing it, I've just been handed a torch, an electrical one, and I'm shining it directly at this thing, and I can see no source for these violent motions. I can only think I am myself witnessing some sort of ... poltergeist activity! Right here in the most mysterious town in Britain! And what it's doing to all these garden gnomes . . . it looks like you had a huge collection, is that right, Sunil?"

"Wherever I went in the world, I found a new one. And I very much regret that now, because—"

"Because almost all of them are . . . on fire? How can gnomes be on fire? Logan, are you seeing this? He's nodding. Sunil, what's doing this?"

"My chef and assistants initially tried to hold them off with brooms, whatever we could find, but I told them to retreat back into the building, because in the end these are just objects, and . . . now you've seen it, I feel we should move back inside, too, because—"

"What's that right there beside us? Is there something there? Hello? Is something trying to communicate? Are you a troubled spirit? Are you causing these people to burn their own homes? What is it that you want to—! Oh, something's tugging on me. Sunil's trying to pull me back, Logan, get back, I'm trying to communicate with . . . no! No! Let go of me! Let go! Ahhhhh!"

(Cue spooky theme music.)

4

AUTUMN AND ZOYA RAN ACROSS TOWN, avoiding the crowds, Zoya managing to tap on her phone as they did so. She got an immediate message back from babysitter Louise, who'd heroically stepped up to cover Zoya's urgent journey. Jas was okay but was asking if soldiers were coming. She'd told Louise she'd be home as soon as she could, but Louise had just told her to go get those gnomes. Which gave Zoya a bitter feeling in her stomach as she pocketed her phone.

Every now and then on their journey, the two would encounter desperate people wanting Autumn's help, but every time Autumn had kept running, calling that they were sorting this. Lizzie was certainly important to Autumn, but Zoya was pretty sure that was a mixture of the closeness of two old friends who'd been through a lot together and Lizzie's usefulness to their magical work. The feelings Lizzie had confided to Zoya just weren't on Autumn's radar

They got to the gateway of the Vicarage to find the gnomes in the garden still blazing with magical flame, and the windows vibrating with cracking impacts as if the building were under small arms fire. "I rip this glamour!" bellowed Autumn, marching forward and throwing her arms wide.

Suddenly, Zoya could see the assailants: a group of half-a-dozen gnomes in black and green overalls, their usual caps in place, but these metallic and burnished. They carried something like slingshots. They spun at the intrusion, and Zoya flinched as something flashed through the air past her.

But Autumn stamped her foot and threw her left palm forward, her fingers clawed in something like a yoga pose. The gnomes jumped back as whatever she'd hurled landed close to them. "You dare to fight the Wise Woman?" yelled Autumn. "I call to all the compass and take the tide to my brow! You want some, do you?!"

In a flash of movement, the gnomes were into the undergrowth and gone.

Autumn just about fell back into Zoya's arms. "Shit," she whispered, "that was all I had. They don't know how much... even the smallest aggressive magic costs. I've pegged it to calories. Which is great, to a point, but... God, I hope Lizzie's got something high protein in her fridge."

Zoya helped her to the door and rang the bell. "How likely is that?"

There was a bustle at the curtain, then Lizzie opened the door. "Oh no," she said. "Come on in, let's get you a toasted tea cake."

Lizzie led them to the kitchen but staggered at the threshold. Zoya saw with horror that she had some sort of small injury on her neck, like a sting. Okay, so, time for her to step in and help these two idiots. Zoya sat them both down at the dining room table and went to grab some sting relief from the disorganized mass of stuff that was the bathroom cabinet. At least there was no noise of gnomes in the garden. Autumn seemed to have scared them off. For now.

"While I was closing the windows," Lizzie was saying, breathing hard, when Zoya returned to the dining room, "one of them got me. Some sort of invisible dart. It sort of... melted when I pulled it out. But... I think there's something in there."

"I'll... I'll do something," said Autumn, "just give me a minute."

Zoya, thinking this unlikely right now, started applying the lotion.

"You shouldn't have come for me—" began Lizzie.

"Shut up," said Autumn. "We need you."

"Do you?"

"Of course we do. Lizzie, for God's sake, this isn't you. What's up with you? I need my old Lizzie back."

"I . . . think she's gone. I think after this is over, I need to . . . go."

"What? Go where?"

"Away. Away from here. You need to find someone else."

"But . . . the Wise Woman and the priest, that's how it's supposed to be."

"Then I'll stop being the priest."

Autumn grabbed Lizzie's hand in both of hers, which made Lizzie look at her with a tremendous pain on her features. "You love being the priest here. Lizzie, please, talk to me."

"I can't. It's not important."

"Your pulse is racing."

"That's . . . normal for me these days."

"What?"

"I think it's . . . anxiety? Full-on panic attacks, a couple of times."

"So that's the problem?"

"Autumn, you can't solve this."

"Well, a doctor could solve this, medicine or therapy or something—"

"Stop it!" Lizzie shouted.

Autumn stared at her.

"I don't think there's anything much in the wound," Zoya said quickly. "It's only like a mosquito bite. In my books it says that 'elf darts' are more of a warning, like bees butting you if you get too close to the hive."

"Yes, thank you, Zoya," said Autumn, her incredulous attention now fixed on Lizzie.

"It was . . . everything that happened. Everything after Judith died," said Lizzie. "I just . . . found that I started to not be able to deal with the simplest things, like a funeral for someone I knew or a wedding for this couple who didn't know anything about—and there was this christening, and they were so happy, and I just got home and . . . I couldn't go out the next day, I was so . . . afraid."

"Why didn't you tell me?" said Autumn, sounding full-on accusing.

Lizzie was silent.

"Ham," said Zoya. "There will be ham in the fridge, and tuna in the cupboard perhaps. And you both need hot tea. Wait there. Maybe not talking." She marched into the kitchen. But something immediately caught her attention. Through the big window looking out onto the driveway she could see the bobbing of new lights. Okay, if the gnomes were back, Autumn was going to need that ham.

But before she could go to the fridge, she heard the

voices. Human voices. They were calling and jeering. Zoya restrained herself from getting a carving knife out of the drawer, went out into the hallway, and threw open the front door.

It was a bunch of the locals. They were holding flaming torches. "There's one of them!" shouted the elderly woman who seemed to be leading them. "They brought this on us! You witches come on out, or we'll burn you all!"

"What the hell are you doing, Sheila?" An elderly man with an incredulous look on his face and an extraordinary abundance of facial hair was marching up the Vicarage drive.

Zoya noted that some of the mob with flaming torches were now looking sheepish and took advantage of the moment. "They were going to burn the vicar!"

"Now, that's an exaggeration—"

"No it weren't, Sheila, you said they were witches and we were going to burn them," said one pensioner in the group who'd obviously decided to distance himself from this whole thing.

"Well . . . yes, but—"

The man, who seemed to be the group's overall leader, had now reached them. "I don't believe this. You went off to find the gnomes, and I don't bloody care what you do to *them*, but you come here, of all the so-called places, to one of our own institutions, to the *Vicarage*—"

"And we'll get to that magic shop, too, they're the ones who started all this," said Sheila, obviously not on-message, and Zoya was worried to see that a handful of her group were nodding along. She knew how these things went. She would wait until they were thoroughly at it and go get that bread knife. "You can't pick and choose with this lot, Jim. They brought all these changes here. We remember what it were like before, when decent folk lived here and you could leave your door open and everyone was . . . was a person!"

"Aren't *we* people?" a voice beside Zoya said. Lizzie had come to the door. With a shaking finger, she switched on the porch light, and suddenly the mob with flaming torches, illuminated, looked more like a group of carol singers.

"And the gnomes are people too," said Autumn, who'd squared up beside Lizzie, obviously a little wary of letting the Reverend take the lead.

"No!" said Sheila, and several others joined in. "No, they aren't. They should be garden gnomes, and that's all. It's the same all over, there's stuff that's always been there, and it's getting ripped out and replaced and nobody asks us old people if it's all right with us. You new people are changing everything—"

"I am not 'new people,'" said Autumn, an undercurrent of barely contained rage in her voice.

"Don't you yell at me!" shouted Sheila. "I belong here!"

"Sheila, stop," said Jim, looking wildly around him, aware that he was holding the attention of barely half the crowd. "This is a distraction. We need to continue the patrols, find the gnomes who are doing this—"

"I want an apology from her, from them, for all of this!" said Sheila.

"You want *what*—?" roared Autumn, taking one step out of the doorway and flinging her arms wide.

"No!" shouted Lizzie and leapt out in front of her as the crowd screamed and stumbled back. "Dearly beloved—!" Lizzie turned as she said it, the words the start of the service that Zoya had heard her preach when she'd married Autumn and Luke, words this crowd would presumably be familiar with. But was she directing them toward them, or to—?

Autumn fumed for a moment, then turned on her heel and marched back inside.

"Yeah," said Sheila, "and don't come back."

"Sheila Lampton," said Lizzie, rounding on her. "I baptised your granddaughter, didn't I? I remember her playing with the flowers on your hat."

"That's right, vicar. I didn't know who you was then."

"Sheila, no," said Jim, shaking his head.

"I don't judge you for what you do this evening," continued Lizzie, sounding to Zoya as if she was just about holding on, but still with the public speaking skills to be the centre of the mob's attention. "But I've seen you come to light a candle. You believe that *someone's* going to judge you. Do you really think you've loved your neighbor tonight?"

"That's the point, Reverend. They're not my neighbrs. Not these new people, not people like your mate, and especially not the bloody elves and gnomes and what have you. You and old Judith and these two brought them here—"

"And the builders," said a man in the crowd. "The builders and the gnomes go way back. I bet they burned that house down just so their mates could charge a fortune to repair it."

"Here, the builders!" said the one who'd distanced himself from Sheila earlier, sounding like he'd found his opportunity. "They can show us where to find the gnomes. What do you reckon, Jim?"

Jim looked relieved to find himself at least nominally back in charge. Zoya could see a political mind making calculations. "Ar," he said after a moment. "Worth a shot. We can join all our parties together and have a word, a *polite* word." He looked awkwardly to Lizzie. "Evening, then, Reverend."

He headed off, looking to see if the mob were following. After a moment's hesitation, they all did. Even Sheila. Who looked back over her shoulder at Lizzie and Zoya and shook her head.

Zoya followed Lizzie as she locked and bolted the door, then marched inside to find Autumn.

The Wise Woman was pacing in the kitchen. "Fucking *racist*—!"

"I know," said Lizzie, "some of them."

"Too many of them," said Zoya. "And not enough spoke up."

Lizzie leaned heavily on the fridge. Zoya saw her fingers checking the pulse in her neck. "But, Autumn, if you'd done anything magic to them, you'd pay for it so much, and you'd hate yourself for doing it and—"

Autumn sounded almost as angry at Lizzie as she had at the mob outside. "I wasn't going to, that was just a feint, to make them—"

"No it wasn't." But before Autumn could reply, Lizzie suddenly dropped into a crouch, breathing hard. "Okay. Okay. I just need to—"

"Oh God, Lizzie," Autumn snapped out of her anger. "We have to get you—"

"No," said Lizzie. "No time, because we just... heard some local lore that... I hadn't heard before. And that's... worrying. But it means... someone's trying to keep something secret."

"What?" said Zoya.

"Like they said outside," said Lizzie. "We need to find a builder."

———

Loz had had an idea, a straw to grasp at as she watched the people of her beloved town go, well, not to put too fine a point on it, apeshit. As the town clerk, she hadn't been under any illusions about what the general public were like, but... actually, maybe she had been under some illusions, because she still couldn't quite believe they were capable of what she'd seen as she and Dave had run through the town. "We need to get to the council offices," she'd told him, and in that moment, as if it were the most natural thing in the world, she'd taken his hand.

"Why?" He'd immediately gone with her, though, and he hadn't let go. His hand had felt big and rough and finely detailed.

"Because maybe these gnomes have been doing recon, but knowing which building they could burn down without inflicting too much misery? That's serious local knowledge."

"Yeah. Yeah, that's brilliant. So—"

They'd run around the corner and now had the council offices in sight, beside the churchyard and the community centre, opposite the beauty salon, and thankfully not showing any sign of being on fire. "They might still be in there, yeah. Oh, there we go." She pointed to the top floor. A single light shone in the window of the back room where the paper records were kept.

They made their way to the door, both of them adopting a sort of stealthy scamper. Loz found her keys and opened the door as quietly as she was able. "They won't hurt us," said Dave.

"You don't sound sure of that."

He just looked grimly at her as they made their way quietly up the stairs. Thankfully, they both knew this place so well they didn't need light. The familiar polish smell of work seemed so odd when their town was on fire. Loz stopped. She could hear voices, speaking a tongue she didn't understand, but, a bit like with the Scandinavian languages, sounded like it might resolve into English at any moment. They were small, high voices, gruff like toddlers being gruff, almost cute. In another context she might have laughed at them. She recalled an article she'd read once about when the ancestors of modern humans had lived on the plains, and they'd evolved to be afraid of other sorts of humans: the bigger ones and the smaller ones. The author had speculated that there was the origin of human mythologies.

Little had they known. She really needed to know how this all worked. How, in the end, their *world* worked. Up until now, horribly, incredibly in retrospect, it hadn't seemed important.

But then Dave was suddenly pounding up the stairs, calling out something she didn't understand—because it was in that same unfamiliar language!

Loz rushed after him, and together they burst through the doorway of the records room. The scene they found there was oddly normal. Someone was at the PC, caught with hand on mouse, another was carrying a pile of paper records, a third was halfway up the steps, reaching for a high filing cabinet drawer. The only odd thing about it was that all those people were gnomes. They had had a moment to prepare themselves, and had chosen, Loz supposed, to stay and glower at them rather than vanish.

Dave said something else in their language. He sounded angry, exasperated, desperate.

The gnome at the PC, who was wearing combat fatigues and a little camouflage cap, hopped down and pointed at him as if he was a blasphemer. He said something short and sharp, and then, in what must have been deliberately researched sign language, made a *V* sign that definitely didn't stand for victory.

The speed with which Dave moved surprised everyone. In one move, he was across the room, had grabbed the gnome, and with a yell, threw him across the room. He hit the wall and fell, and the other gnomes cried out in shock.

Loz was pretty bloody shocked herself. "No," she said, and moved to help the gnome, but Dave actually grabbed her arm and held her back, until she shook him off because she wasn't bloody having that.

"It's ... it's okay," he said. "They're tougher than us." Sure enough, Loz was relieved to see the gnome slowly getting to his feet. But it wasn't as if he wasn't injured. His nose looked broken, and he was holding his chest like he'd broken some ribs. "You broke your oath too," said Dave to the gnome. "I thought I could trust you not to overreact. We all did." Now he sounded like he regretted what he'd done. But he obviously couldn't let go of his anger.

Shaking, but looking more furious than ever, the gnome put a hand to his belt and pulled out a dagger. Loz turned at the sound of the other two drawing their weapons too. "He doesn't speak for me," she said quickly. "I represent the council, not the elected ones who sent you that message but the workers who are always here, whose job it is to help everyone. I'm sorry he did that. I want to negotiate."

"Too late for that," said Dave. He sounded like he was blaming the gnomes, and Loz suddenly felt angry at herself for falling for such a bloody fool.

The gnomes rushed at them, yelling.

Loz had a moment of absolute fear as Dave tried to get between them and her. She had time to think what it would be like to have a knife cut into her. She had never felt such extremity, had never been in a situation where harm was right on her, right on top of her.

Then the window seemed to fold in on itself, and the gnomes were all suddenly, impossibly, flying out of it with a great rush of air, screaming as they went. In front of Loz and Dave landed Autumn Blunstone, her sort-of-a-coat-with-a-scarf-maybe-attached flowing like water, the walls rippling themselves closed behind her with a decisive slam. Beside her had also landed that new one, Zoya, mimicking Autumn's perfect three-point impact, and the Reverend Lizzie, who fell on her face on the carpet. "Good thing you chose here," Autumn said after a moment, out of breath. "I put a lot of power into this place's defenses years back." She looked to Dave. "And good thing you're here too. We were looking for a builder."

Autumn spent a few minutes making sure the defenses of the council offices were holding steady, that there were no more gnomes in the building, and that they wouldn't be disturbed here, while Lizzie, having picked herself up, had sat Dave and Loz down and made them tea. Autumn watched, sidelong, saw Lizzie's hands shaking, saw how Zoya stepped in to carry things. Damn it, what was *wrong* with Lizzie? Why had she not once mentioned it to her, when Autumn was meant to be her closest friend? Right now the town needed all three of them at their best. At least Lizzie was on the tea tonight rather than the filthy flavored coffees she normally drank. All that caffeine couldn't be good for those shaky hands.

"Thanks for helping us," Dave said, having taken a few moments to compose himself. "What I did just then... it was pretty counterproductive."

"It was escalation," said Loz, sounding angry with him.

Dave paused for a moment but obviously decided not to address that. "And we interrupted their research about the houses, which also maybe wasn't the best idea, in hindsight."

"You can't say I'm as much to blame as—"

"I'm not. I just mean that now they might not pick their targets so carefully. And yes, it was escalation, and that is my fault. Maybe all of this is my fault."

Autumn saw Loz's expression soften. Hey, was something going on between these two? She was always the last to realize this stuff. "I think you should tell us all you know, both about yourself and about why certain people in this town think builders and gnomes are connected."

"They really seem to be," said Loz, and she told them about how Dave had been speaking the gnome language, and how he'd referred to the gnomes also breaking promises. "What was it you think they overreacted to?" she asked him, studying his face. "What don't I know about you?"

"Just start any time," said Zoya, "whenever you can get a word in."

"When I was ten years old," said Dave, "I got lost in the woods. And I must have wandered over one of these borders of yours. Which were still in place back then. I ended up in the Land of the Gnomes."

Oh no. Autumn closed her eyes for a moment, very aware of what he must have gone through. "How long were you gone?"

"A week. Their time and our time. They do something that keeps it at the same speed. I think about it now, about my poor mum and dad... but I was ten and I played in the woods all the time and I wasn't afraid. My parents got the police out, people combing the woods. Old Judith knocked at our door and said she was going to find me, come what may, and it were at times like that that everyone was pleased to see old Judith."

"How did the gnomes treat you?" asked Lizzie.

"They were great, honestly. I saw them from a distance at first, hid and watched them, followed them to one of their villages. Then this family found me, the dad and all his sons."

"Only one woman amongst them," said Zoya. "This explains a lot."

"The Groench family. They gave me some food, and then asked me how I was going to pay for it. I saw they had all these stones lying around, and they were making a house with them, so I pitched in, did a bit of drystone walling, because my dad had taught me. They were amazed I could lay brick on brick. They started clapping and said I'd paid my debt and they brought the king to see. The old king, this was. When the king realized I'd seen them before they'd seen me, he got all serious and said it was obvious I was a master builder, because I could see gnomes without them deliberately revealing themselves. He took me back to his council chamber and fumbled around in some boxes until he found what he were after. It was a gold trowel, not literally gold, like, but shining like it. The king said it would always lay stones in balance and make me a success in life. He gave it to me, but said if I wanted to keep it, I had to do something for them in return. And I listened and agreed and at that point Judith marched in and started giving him a right tongue-lashing, and a few minutes later she was dragging me off home."

"That sounds like her," said Lizzie sadly.

"This is how it's supposed to work," said Autumn, "the other races like doing deals. The gnomes were known for making straightforward ones."

"Oh ah," said Dave. "No tricks."

"Do you still have this trowel?" said Zoya.

"It's in the van somewhere. I don't like to use it when there's other people on-site, you know. Bit flashy."

Loz interrupted them all, urgent. "What did you say you'd do for them in return?!"

"It's . . . it's a bit personal. I told the old king it might take me a long time to get round to it and he said at the time that was fine, that they wouldn't get impatient. That's why I think they're overreacting, because he promised that. But I'm guessing that bit weren't written down. And now it must be looking to them like I might not get round to it."

"*What is it?*"

He sighed. "I promised to name my firstborn after that king I met."

"Oh," said Loz, looking slightly flustered in a way which Autumn found charming but made Dave look embarrassed. "Is it . . . some sort of complicated gnome name?"

"It's . . . Kev."

"Oh," said Autumn and the others, just about at once.

The expression on Loz's face was now a poised mixture of emotions that could fall in any one of several different directions. "Maybe they think you're ... reluctant to settle down? Possibly because you don't like the name?"

"You'd have to ask them," said Dave, standing up. "Anyway, that's what one of the gnomes' demands is all about. That's the old promise that hasn't been kept."

"You haven't told us the other part," said Lizzie. "About what builders and gnomes have to do with each other. From the sound of your experiences, there's a lot going on there."

"Well, there's others knows more about that than I do. I know the best man to ask, though. And I reckon I know exactly where to find him."

5

SERGEANT SHAUN MAWSON of the Gloucester Constabulary was well aware of the reputation that his hometown of Lychford had amongst the surrounding towns. As the son of the previous Wise Woman, Judith, he'd always known it was all true. When he'd joined the police force he'd made the decision to keep silent about all of it, but following the extraordinary events of that day when the end of the world had seemed just around the corner, and with increasing seniority in his job, he'd begun to be a bit more open. So, when on a training weekend or in the sort of pub where coppers hung out, when after a couple pints, the questions started—"Is there anything to it, then?"—he would now say yes. He'd started, while never committing anything to email, to inform his fellow officers of what they needed to know.

So when his new police station in Lechlade had got the word about multiple incidents in Lychford, he'd been able to just tip a wink to his guv'nor and get assigned to lead the response. Some of that had been about co-ordinating with Mickey and the fire crew, but they knew their business. What Shaun had felt was most urgent was to find Autumn, Lizzie, and Zoya. He'd got, after he'd dropped Autumn a line, a quick WhatsApp briefing from her about what was going on, but it had mostly consisted of him being told to stay in his lane and look after the locals. So he'd sent the copper he'd driven over with, PC Lila Boxton, to do crowd control around the fire, and had started asking around the folk who knew they could talk to him about "local matters."

He'd just got to the stage where his eyebrows had climbed about as far up his forehead as they could go when Sunil Mehra came running up, in a right state. "Thank goodness you're here," he said. "I have an injured celebrity on my premises."

Maybe it was the word "celebrity" that made PC Boxton come trotting over. "Want me to call it in, boss?"

Shaun saw a warning look from Sunil. "Let's ... ah, ascertain the nature of the injuries first."

They found two young men sitting in Sunil's back garden beside the remains of ornamental toadstools. They displayed severe bruising and contusions to the face. They were being tended to by one of the restaurant's employees. "Is that the celebrity then?" asked Boxton, sounding disappointed.

"This is Robin Daniels," said Sunil, "and Logan."

"None the wiser," said Boxton.

As they drew closer, Shaun could hear that Daniels was whispering as he stared at the ground. He was repeating something. "It's all true."

"Good evening, sir," said Shaun. "What's all true, then?"

"Gnomes," said Daniels. "Poltergeists, UFOs, headless horsemen, lake monsters, Bigfoot, alien black cats. Everything we cover in our show."

"Bit of a mixed bag, there, sir. I'd say five out of seven. Probably not UFOs." He realized Daniels, Logan, and Boxton were all staring at him incredulously. "That's just my opinion, mind you. Informed by satellite TV. I was attempting to be reassuring." He cleared his throat and let Boxton through to do a proper medical once-over. Better she do that before asking about the perpetrators. That'd give Shaun time to work out if he was going to induct her in the circle of local coppers who knew the truth.

"There's a job on *Test Match Special*," said the sound engineer, Logan, as he was being encouraged to extend his limbs and report any pain. "All they have to worry about is pigeons and cake."

"I would never have put you in danger," said Daniels, "if I'd ever, ever, thought what we cover was ... true. Oh

God. How can I have been such a hypocrite?"

Shaun was genuinely fascinated to be here for this crisis of conscience. As someone who'd been immersed in this stuff since birth, he'd listened to the occasional episode of Daniels' show and now he felt the presenter was being a bit hard on himself. "If I may say so, sir, you always portrayed yourself as an agnostic, and always seemed to treat everyone with kindness."

"Well, I'm an agnostic no longer. I know what I saw. We were attacked by gnomes, Constable. Yes, you heard that right."

"This callout has everything," said Boxton.

"From now on, no more sceptics, just believers, with me supporting their stories with every resource I can muster. It'll be a hell of a task, convincing the BBC that the need for balance is over, but yeah, yeah, you're right, Sergeant, the world must be told."

"Now, hold on, sir—"

"Logan, if you'll ride with me one last time, now we're aware, we'll be more able to defend ourselves. Come on, we have to cover this. You know we do."

The lad called Logan closed his eyes and finally nodded. "I want the sort of references that'd get me onto *Gardeners' Question Time*."

Daniels got to his feet. "Yeah, the story of this town has to be told. I said it's all true, but this is the place where it's... truest." He looked to Sunil. "You locals have suffered in silence too long. We need scientists down here, or, no, mystics, anyone and everyone who can help. And *Unworldly* can be the fulcrum for that, a shout out to the whole world."

"So these new customers would be from... Bristol? London?" So far Shaun had managed to walk a professional tightrope exactly poised between pleased and worried, but then he was sure his face fell. "Glastonbury?"

But Robin Daniels wasn't listening. "Come on, Logan," he said, helping his sound engineer gather his equipment. "We'll follow the crowd. Shape this story. Stay with it until the shattering climax."

And with a nod to Shaun and Boxton, and a blithe assumption they weren't going to be detained to give a witness statement, they were heading off. Shaun wondered if he might have rather put his foot in it there.

"Now," said Sunil, "we will have more tourists to add to this mess." He gathered his staff and stamped off inside. So no chance of a spot of Bombay Aloo tonight, then.

Boxton looked to Shaun expectantly. "What's the word, Sarge? Do we call it in about the gnomes?"

Shaun shook his head. "Let's deal with what we can deal with and leave the gnomes to the specialists."

"Who's that, then, sir? The Gnome Office?"

"I'll pretend I didn't hear that," said Shaun.

Lizzie was glad that they all followed Dave and Loz at a run, out of the council offices, through the chaos that was still enveloping the town as the church clock chimed 11 p.m., and down Howard Street to the Station Inn. The exercise allowed her to breathe as fast as her anxiety demanded. She kept inwardly urging herself to keep it together and was finding a moment here and there to focus on prayer, but she couldn't find any solid mental ground to stand on. As the town was falling apart, so was she. And she had no idea what she could do to stop it. She had so many self-care leaflets on her desk back at the Vicarage that she gave out to other people, and every time she had tried to apply any of their advice to herself, she had always failed.

She was failing Autumn now by being awkward and distant and not being the partner-in-danger she needed.

They reached the Station Inn. The interior lights were on but the door was closed and the beer garden was without illumination. It seemed to have been spared any gnome attacks, maybe because there weren't any garden ornaments. Dave ran to the door and pounded on it, and after a moment and the noise of many bolts, Owen

Trafalgar flung it open. He looked ready for war.

"Is Paul in there?" asked Dave.

"Of course he is," sighed Owen. "He and Mick are treating it like a lock-in."

Lizzie had to take a moment to lean on the doorway as the others ran in to the back bar. She watched Owen locking up again. Then he looked to her and saw... well, he must have seen how lost she appeared. "Are you okay?" he asked.

She found she couldn't answer. And then suddenly she could. "I... we've hardly met, and I know I shouldn't compare my situation to yours, and we're in the middle of... but there's... there's someone—"

"Reverend." He took a careful step toward her. "Where's this going?"

She just burst into tears.

He paused only a moment, then folded her into his arms. She stayed there, helpless. "I just... stress... anxiety—"

"And for some reason you wanted to tell me because—?"

She took in a deep breath through her nose and still couldn't say. She felt so utterly humiliated and lost, to find comfort only in the arms of a stranger.

"Only it sounded for a moment there like you were coming out to me."

Lizzie was seized by uncertainty. "Did you say 'coming out' or 'coming on'?"

He took a step back. "Oh God, you weren't—I mean, you know... I'm gay, and like you said we don't know each other and—"

"No, no! It was coming out, it was coming out!"

And suddenly he was holding her again. "Oh. Oh my poor love. Is there someone you like?"

"Yes."

"Does she know?"

"No."

"You come and talk to me. After all this is over."

"I will. Thank you. You smell amazing."

"Then at least tonight isn't a total loss."

After a few moments for Lizzie to tidy herself up, they headed into the back bar, to see Paul and his mate Mick, clearly several pints in, looking defensively at Dave. "Stop denying it," Dave was saying. "This lot know, all right? They need to. I've told them about what happened to me when I was a kid. They know there's a connection."

Paul put down his pint, annoyed. "All right, since it's these three asking, and with all that's going on tonight... I s'pose it wouldn't be right to keep schtum any longer. You see, us builders have always been able to see gnomes, like some people see ghosts, like old Judith used to see every bloody thing—excuse my French, Reverend—"

Lizzie almost felt comforted by the old annoyance of people thinking they couldn't swear around her. "It's fine."

"There they were, every now and then, on-site, tutting at a half-arsed job, letting out long, whistling breaths at some cowboy not getting his scaffolding right. But after the rain came and gave all of us the power of the sight, well, then they was everywhere. The local builders worked out some of them were starting to live in New Builds, particularly when it was someone from outside moving in and they couldn't see them. A few of us had a word with a few of them, and from what they told us, they're doing that to make adjustments, because they're worried that what's built here, now the borders have come down, could affect what goes on in their own land, feng shung like."

"Feng shui," said Mick.

"Bless you," said Paul.

Lizzie could see how that might work, given the Sovo supermarket chain's evil plan to destabilise the borders around Lychford that had first brought Lizzie into all this, so many years ago. "Why did you keep all this to yourselves?" she asked.

"Yeah," said Autumn, "this is pretty vital information."

"We're used to keeping stuff close to our chests. We're craftsmen, all right? And craft doesn't get a lot of respect these days. So if we know summat it stays as summat we know, and if anyone else needs to know, they should know already. We especially didn't like to talk about the gnomes, because outside of Lychford that's a good way of losing your six months of putting a new wing on some toff's mansion."

"Do you have a red book?" said Zoya. "About this big. *The Red Book of the Build*. Or is that not a thing here like it is in Ukraine?"

Paul looked astonished. "How do you know about that?"

"My dad, he was a builder. And his father. He wanted me to carry on, but . . . a ridiculous man led me here instead. But I've seen the red book, with my father and his friends."

Paul looked like he'd been caught out. Lizzie wondered how many more secrets he wasn't telling them. "Over here," he said, "it's called *The Red Book of Grout*." He went to where his jacket and Hi-Viz were folded on a stool and took something from the pocket of the latter.

"Since the gnomes started playing up, I've been keeping it with me." He opened it up and Lizzie saw very fine handwritten pages. "When one of these wears out, you have to copy it out in a new notebook. It's an encyclopedia, really. Alphabetical."

"Is there an entry about the war memorial?" said Loz. "That's the part of the gnomes' demands we still don't understand."

Paul flipped through the book and failed to find anything of the kind under *W*. Lizzie was suddenly struck by a thought. "Try 'sounding true,'" she said, "or anything about sounds. That always seemed like odd wording to me. If they felt what was written on the war memorial was deliberately wrong wouldn't they just say 'lying'?"

Paul flipped the pages again, and a worried look came over his face. "Oh," he said.

They all crowded to look over his shoulder. "Lizzie," said Autumn, "you're back in the game."

Lizzie felt ridiculously pleased and hated that feeling in the same moment. There it was on the page:

> "**Song:** *Certain other folk of the different worlds have it that they hear construction as a song. Summon a gnome (see appendices) and ask if your build sounds true.*"

"So," said Autumn, "it's not what's written on the monument that's wrong. It's the monument itself. The way it's built."

"But hasn't it been here since 1918?" said Zoya. "Why this grievance now?"

"Because it were renovated in the 2000s," said Paul. "And it were moved, ever so slightly, to get it out the way of where the County Council wanted to lay a pipe. I should know. It were one of my jobs."

"Hi, I'm Robin Daniels of the *Unworldly* podcast, and as you're listening to this now, myself and my brave sound engineer, Logan—can't get even a nod out of him tonight, which is understandable, value your work anyway, Logan—we're running. We're running across the still blazing ruin—"

"They've just about put it out now."

"Yes, thank you, Logan, I believe that's your first contribution to an episode. That might stick out a bit. We might have to edit that out. We're running through the embattled town of Lychford, which is under attack, and I don't think that's overstating the case, under attack by what I can only describe as... gnomes. Yes, you heard that right, common or garden, in most cases garden, gnomes are in the streets here, they're invisible, they're setting buildings alight, and I have seen them with my own eyes. I know in the past this was a series about scepticism and belief, that I always tried to walk a fine line, but now... I have seen them with my own eyes."

"You might have to edit around you saying they were invisible."

"And a second contribution! Yes, thank you, Logan. Anyway, we're sprinting now, and you can probably hear the fear in our voices, because—oh, I should really insert this here—"

(Cue spooky theme music.)

"—and up ahead I can see now, we're catching up to the local vicar and the staff of the magic shop we interviewed earlier, and the landlord of the pub where I'm staying, and I think that's the mayor and there's the town clerk, and here are two men I don't recognize, one, balding, slim, mid-seventies—"

"Hoi!"

"Oh, hi—they've stopped and are looking at us perhaps a little angrily—I'm Robin Daniels of the *Unworldly* podcast—"

"Oh, you're him! Well, if this is going out on the radio, hello to my nieces Candice and Brandy, and mid-sixties if you please."

"He'll get his shirt off if you're not careful."

"We've been joined by another middle-aged, balding—"

"Now you've gone and spoiled it."

"Cut to the chase, literally. Can I ask, what are two gentlemen such as yourselves, the vicar, the landlord, the mayor, the town clerk, and the magic shop people all doing running across town in the middle of the night?"

"Isn't it obvious? Local marathon."

"No, listen, I've seen the gnomes. I know it's all true. Ah, here comes Autumn, the owner of the magic shop. Autumn, listen, you're now talking to a believer."

"Then you should know it's in everyone's best interest if you get the fuck out of the way and let us get on with our business."

"And they're off again. And we're running with them. Autumn, Autumn, you can't be hoping to keep this place a secret anymore, can you? The rumours are already worldwide, and when this episode goes out, with perhaps our highest ever listening figures, and I'm now thinking spinoff TV show on at least BBC Two, it'll be absolutely clear to everyone what a terrifying place this town of yours is—oh, and the vicar's stopped, do you want to engage with that, Reverend Lizzie?"

"It is not terrifying! It's a wonderful place to live. With wonderful people. And by people I don't just mean human beings. This place is good. Good earth. A good place to be. I'm glad I took the job back here—"

"Well, I didn't expect an essay—"

"And if our story is going to go out to the world, it will make Autumn and Zoya and me saving that world on a regular basis a lot more bloody difficult. So . . . just think about that!"

"And she's off again. The other two are reaching out to her, holding her hand, that's nice to see. But something has occurred to me. When she said 'saving the world . . .' Was that literal? Is everything they say about this place true? Is a small market town in Gloucestershire the scene of battles in which our very existence as a species is at stake? Oh, and talking of battles, everyone's slowing down . . . let's take a moment to get our breath back and take this in, because up ahead I'm seeing . . . everyone seems to have been running to the marketplace, and a crowd up ahead has formed around the war memorial. They've got . . . even with all that's happened to their buildings tonight they're still carrying the flaming torches. I'm seeing some rakes and brooms, lengths of pipe, and a few cricket bats. And one of them . . . oh my God, one of them has a shotgun. This is getting serious."

"You reckon?"

"Thank you, sir, can I get your name?"

"Just call me the balding seventies one."

"And at the head of the group around the war memorial, defending it, presumably from the gnomes, there's that councillor, I believe Jim is his name, and he seems to be addressing them."

"The wanker."

"We're going to have to edit that out, but thanks for that contribution, Mr. Anonymous. Oh, and Autumn's coming back to us. Hello, Autumn, what do you want to say to us?"

"Maybe there's something you can actually do here. Paul here—"

"Ah, so that's his name. Hello, Paul."

"He needs to get to that war memorial and do some building work."

"Oh come on now, I thought we were past the point of you people telling lies to—"

"I'm telling you this is true. If you're famous, if some of those people will have heard your programme, and you probably do get higher listening figures in Lychford than anywhere else, you need to go and address that crowd and get them to let Paul through so he can make right whatever's wrong with that thing."

"Oh. Bloody hell, Autumn—"

"Not that it'll be obvious. He says he's going to consult the red book—"

"It'll take time and all. Job where you don't know what's gone wrong is the worst job of all."

"And we're heading up to midnight and the gnomette said we should fear that moment. So, will you do it? Will you speak to them for us?"

"Listeners, what else can I do? It's going to require great personal courage on my part, but... I figure I'm part of the story now. So. Logan, I can't ask you to come with me. You stay here and narrate what happens to me. Okay... you're listening to *Unworldly*, perhaps for the last time, and... bloody hell, here I go."

(Cue spooky theme music.)

Autumn watched as Robin Daniels slowly approached the crowd around the war memorial, his hands raised entirely theatrically, as if he were a Shakespearean actor brokering peace between Romulans and Klingons. Now there was a metaphor straight from Lizzie. Autumn remembered the evening she'd flopped down on the Vicarage sofa and had said, "Okay, subject me to it," and had been shown some TV episodes the context of which seemed wildly complicated but which Lizzie had delighted in explaining to her.

She looked sidelong now and was again struck by the comparison between Lizzie's animated features on that night barely a year ago and how she was now. Older. They all felt older. The events of the last few years had stressed out the entire human race, but the inhabitants of Lychford had had their own extra and impossible terrors on top. And here was the damage from that exploding all around them, a chaotic chain reaction of fear. It seemed to have taken Lizzie worst of all, for reasons Autumn still didn't fully understand, and instead of standing up herself, here she was, the supposed Wise Woman, sending this ridiculous podcast host to do her job for her.

She was still wrestling with whether or not she should step forward, too, or if that would be counterproductive, when he started to speak. "People of Lychford. Many of you know me. I'm Robin Daniels, host of the *Unworldly* podcast. Do we have any listeners in? Ah, I see we do. Hi. I'm not here to loom at you. I'm told I sometimes loom. Sorry. Where was I? Yes. Please could you lower that shotgun? Thanks. Appreciate that. Now, in recent years, I've become not just an expert in, but a witness to, the unworldly. This we're all experiencing tonight, and similar things you've experienced here, because I'm sure about the nature of this place now... this is unworldly. And of course, you want it to stop? Right? Yeah, I see you nodding back there, sir. Of course you do."

Autumn began to feel her initial instincts about this might have been correct after all. The man did have a way with a crowd. Or, as she was sure he thought of them, an audience. "We're here to defend what's ours!" shouted Jim, seemingly realising that his place as idiot-being-listened-to was being usurped. "We're not letting them cancel our past!"

"Of course you're not! Yeah! Onside with that!" called Robin.

"I have nightmares like this," muttered Owen Trafalgar. "I never thought I'd see a mob here, but just scratch the surface of this town—"

"A lot of them are good people," said Loz. "They'll come round. Even Jim."

"We saw," said Lizzie, her eyes closed, her hands clasped together, seemingly praying, "that there's good in Jim. In all of them."

"But what are we really looking at here?" continued Robin. "A message from powers we don't understand. What do we say when we're sitting in a séance? Is there anyone there? Well, clearly there is tonight. And we don't know what they're trying to say."

"Yes you do!" called a small, high-pitched voice from the trees at the edge of the church grounds. "We keep telling you! That monument must be made to sound true!"

The crowd roared in anger. The man with the shotgun swung to aim it toward the trees until a woman who was probably his wife beside him put her hand on his shoulder. But still he didn't lower the weapon. "It's true for us!" yelled Jim. "You can't erase those names!

You can't change history!"

"Why," called Robin, as if joining in, "do you want to?"

And the crowd joined in with him, asking the same question. But if there was an answer, it was drowned out by their cries, the question swiftly becoming rhetorical.

"Before midnight!" called the voice at the end of whatever it had been saying. "Before the moment when the stars fix it for another month. We won't stand it a moment more! If you don't sort this by then, everything burns!"

"I can do it!" shouted Paul, stepping forward. "Just give me a hand and a bag of tools and I can start the job, at least, though I dunno if I'll get it done before midnight. And if the gnomes will tell me what to do, I'll—!"

Someone in the crowd threw a rock. It caught him on the shoulder and he fell with a cry.

"Bastards!" shouted Zoya, running to help him. "He's one of you, he's an old man!"

"Oi," said Paul from the ground. Mick was already helping him to his feet, looking furious. "I'm in my prime." But the look on his face said that more than his pride and his shoulder had been hurt.

"Get the gnomes!" shouted someone in the crowd.

"But then who will defend the memorial?!" called Robin. "It's a real dilemma!"

"I might start listening to his show," said Dave.

"Proper job he's doing."

"We don't care for our own lives," called the little voice from the bushes. "We've brought wrecking tools. If that eyesore's not fixed in the next half hour we'll demolish it. One of us will get through."

"Now, I'm used to arbitrating, between believers and sceptics," began Robin, "so—"

"We will never surrender!" bellowed Jim.

And the crowd joined in, starting to shout, over and over, "Gnomes out!"

But then, from the road behind Autumn and her team, came the noise of marching feet. Autumn turned to see a small group of locals in anoraks approaching, carrying torches of the electrical kind and signs that said *Protect the gnomes* and *Non-Human Rights*. They were led by that councillor, Matt Coomby, who had a determined look on his face. "We are here," he called, pointing toward the war memorial, "to defend our non-human visitors from prejudice and intimidation!"

The crowd around the memorial yelled back at him. "What about our rights?" shouted Jim.

"You've all got until midnight to sort yourselves out and step away from that edifice!" called the voice from the bushes. "Then we charge!"

Robin Daniels looked back over his shoulder to Autumn. "Phew," he said. "Tough audience."

6

JAS BOYKO WAS TEN, and she knew everything. Her mum, Zoya, had told her she was going to spend today with Nanny Louise, and that was great, because Louise had more time for Jas' Lego builder videos than Mum did, and she had a carpet with a pattern of squares on it. Jas would walk along the lines of the squares, counting them, and they made sixty-four, Louise said, except Jas disagreed because there was the sofa over part of them, so she didn't know. Louise always laughed when Jas said that, but she told her it was a nice laugh, and otherwise she made sure to talk about things as they were and not about how they could be or weren't, and that made Jas feel good. They always had the same snacks and the same TV shows in the same order when Jas came to stay.

But today, and especially tonight, had been a bit different. There had been noises from the town, so Louise had turned the sound on the TV up for CBBC before bedtime at 8:30 p.m. Then, when Jas had gone up to her sometimes bedroom with the covers that smelled different but okay, the noises had got worse and there had been lights, and when Jas had got out of bed to go and find Louise, Louise had met her on the stairs and said Jas could come downstairs and wrap up on the sofa with her and they could watch some quiz shows together. Jas had asked if it was the Russians outside. Louise had had an odd look on her face, but had told her simply no, it wasn't, it was some people being silly, and it would all be over in time for school in the morning.

So that was okay. But as they watched the quiz shows, the noises had got louder and the sudden lights had got nearer.

Jas jumped now as there was a knock on the door. But she quickly realized it had gone "knock diddly knock knock," and that sounded friendly, not like Russians.

Louise smoothed her head and went to answer it, keeping the chain on the door. Then she opened it and in came Autumn's husband, Luke, fake smiling. Jas never liked it when adults did that. "Hey, Jas," he said. "How are you?"

Jas knew that Autumn and Luke giving them some money was why her mum was able to have Nanny Louise look after her, and she knew they were friends, but she was very worried Luke was here to take her away. "Where's Mummy?"

"She's out with Autumn and Lizzie, helping people." And now he sounded better. He'd squatted down by the sofa, and his smile had become a real one. "Autumn texted me and asked me to come here and make sure you two were okay."

"We're okay," said Louise. "They haven't come anywhere near, really. How's Autumn doing?"

"No idea, I just go where I'm told. Knowing her, she's giving them hell. If that's an appropriate turn of phrase." Jas liked how Luke talked about Autumn.

"I've been keeping track of the town Facebook page," said Louise. "Is all of what they're saying true?"

"Knowing that lot, probably not. But there are ... bad guys out there, and an old house has been set on fire, but there was nobody in it. People have been hurt, but that's it so far."

Jas didn't like it when she heard something weird going on in the way adults talked. "Bad guys," she said.

"Right," said Luke. He looked at Louise in a strange way again, as if something was being said or was being asked without them using words.

"I don't like those demands they made," said Louise. "It's no business of theirs what we do with our war memorial, is it? And they should be flattered about the garden gnomes."

"There's more to it," said Luke. "I ... kind of see where they're coming from about the garden gnomes. If you put yourself in their shoes."

"Well now I don't feel like doing that," said Louise. "I mean, I've got garden gnomes, and they weren't meant to offend anybody, they don't even—"

There came a sudden noise from the garden. "You've got garden gnomes?" said Luke.

Louise got a weird look on her face. "Okay, Jas," she said, gathering up the duvet Jas had brought down to the sofa. "We're going to go into the back room now, all of us together—"

The noise in the garden suddenly became huge, like thunder, and there was a flash of red light, right there outside, illuminating the curtains. Louise had stepped between Jas and the glass, but Jas still saw the flash so brightly it stayed in her eyelids after she closed them. "Okay," said Luke. "I've got keys to the magic shop, they can't get in there, Autumn's got defenses up. We can run out the back—"

"I'm not risking that," said Louise.

There came a sudden rattle of small things hitting the windows.

Jas stood up and walked to the square pattern on the carpet. She started to pace it. "Is she okay?" said Luke.

"It's just what she does," said Louise. "It calms her down. And okay, maybe we should—"

"North and south, east and west," said Jas under her breath, taking care not to stumble with the words. "I call on Taylor and Jin and Dua and Harry." And she used some words from Mummy's old language before they came to the UK. "Walls and walls and walls and walls. Fours and fours and fours and fours." Then she had to say something very difficult and make herself think about something difficult, but this was one of those times when it was good to make herself stretch and feel like inside her head was doing too much. "And ... under the sofa too!" She stopped, turned, made the bows, scrunched her fists.

Suddenly, the noises at the window stopped.

She looked up at Luke and Louise. They had weird expressions again. "Chip off the old block," said Luke.

Zoya had to close her eyes. When she'd been younger, before Jas had come along, she'd spent some time in the towns to the east of her home country, communities where sympathies had lain more with Moscow than with Kyiv. She'd listened to the talk in the coffee bars there, and what she'd heard had made her close her eyes in just the same way as she was now. There was something about people, she thought, not even just about human beings but about gnomes, too, where they seemed only able to choose one thing out of two. Us and them. Good and evil. The latter assigned to the former. Everything that was in between, everything awkward, got shoved into one of the two camps. And doing that distorted the real world, destroyed all hope of finding what was actually true, if that truth was a problem for the tribe you'd chosen. "Can you even hear yourselves?" she said, too quietly, she thought, for anyone to hear above all the shouting.

"No," said Lizzie, "they can't." Zoya opened her eyes and saw Lizzie visibly taking a series of deep breaths. "I'm going to walk Paul to the war memorial. Let's see if they'll attack a priest."

"Right you are," said Paul, with a visible gulp.

Zoya couldn't be allowing this. She put a hand on Lizzie's arm, holding her back. "They will attack a priest," she said. "And then they will have attacked a priest, and they will be unable to walk back from that, so they'll keep on doubling down. You do not want to live in a town where they've attacked a priest."

"Then what—?!" It had begun as a shout from Lizzie. But then she quietened herself. "What good am I?"

"I don't know why you're asking that, vicar, when none of us have been at our best," said Dave. "I attacked one of that lot, the gnomes I mean, when they were alright to me as a kid, when I should have spent my life building those bridges, not ignoring everything I'd been through. If I'd done that, we'd all be in a much better place. Maybe there wouldn't even have been the need for you lot to do all you have over the last few years." He turned to Loz. "I owe you an apology and all. You tried to tell me just that, to choose the better way. You were after keeping me on the straight and narrow."

Loz looked flustered. "I . . . I just want everyone to be okay."

"So I should be the one to go over there with Paul," said Dave. "It's my responsibility, being the mayor—"

"Right-ho," said Paul, again girding his loins.

"What I said about priests," said Zoya, "applies to mayors too."

"Wise Woman here," said Autumn. "Well done with all the self-sacrifice, but sacrificing things is my job. If I can just get a minute to pull myself together, maybe I can just shove all of them back and—"

"And then you'll have a full-on riot," said Robin Daniels, jogging back from where he'd been regarding the standoff between rival protestors and the unseen gnomes. "For God's sake, look at them. Have none of you people had media training?"

"Not a priority round here," said Mick.

"Well, listen, with Logan's help here, I'm going to livecast whatever happens next, because dramatic countdown to midnight. Maybe it'll hold some of those people accountable. Just try to make it good radio."

"That," said Autumn, "will not be much of a priority either."

"Maybe I should just get over there on my own?" said Paul, visibly tiring at all the false starts. "I mean, it's five minutes to midnight, someone's got to do summat." He looked to Zoya. "Does what you said apply to builders?"

"Not so much, honestly," said Zoya.

"No, stop it. What Dave just said, we need to build a bridge," said Lizzie, grabbing them all by the hands, as much as even her big hands could do that, trying to pull them all in. They all rather tried to join in. "And do you remember, Autumn, what I said, that back in the day Judith once told me gnomes could build things in people's dreams and imaginations? Well, I've just thought, that's what I've been trying to do with my anxiety attacks—"

"Which I could have helped you with if you'd—" began Autumn.

"—build myself a calmness," said Lizzie, cutting her off. "If calm were a building, what sort of building would it be?"

"A pub or a greenhouse," said Mick. Then he saw their expressions. "Sorry."

"I see that building in my mind," said Lizzie, "I put it there, visualise it, when I need something to support myself. Strong and steadfast and undemanding. That's what I've kept saying it's like. That could look like a bridge, couldn't it?"

"Bridges don't ask much of people, true," said Paul.

"If we put that to the gnomes," said Lizzie, "if we let them know that we'd use your magic, Autumn, to make that visualisation work at our end, maybe they could, you know, help to build calm here?"

"That... could actually work," said Autumn.

"And with my help, maybe they could make the war memorial sound right and all," said Paul. "I've got the plans for just about everything I've built somewhere in the back of my noggin."

"But how do we talk to the gnomes?" said Zoya. "How do we get past all the shouting?"

"That's my job," said Dave. "I can buy us enough time to deliver that message."

He made to go, but Loz grabbed his hand. "I'm coming with you," she said.

Zoya saw Dave look at her like she'd just saved his life. He gave her an awkward smile and nodded. "Oh ah," he said. "Let's be off, then."

And a moment later they were.

"You're brilliant," Autumn said to Lizzie.

"I'm an idiot," said Lizzie, looking back at her with the same sort of expression that had been on Dave's face a moment ago.

But again, Zoya saw Autumn completely missing it.

Loz was summoning all of what was turning out to be her considerable courage to walk with Dave toward the undergrowth. She was looking into the faces of people she knew screaming at her, people she'd been polite to in her office picking up stones ready to throw at her. Others were stepping into their way and screaming right back at them. Whatever her expression in return might be seemed an utterly futile question. There was no emotion she could summon that could handle this. So after having seen some of those faces, she looked behind her, and saw Autumn huddling with her two friends, making gestures, probably trying to find some spell for calm, while Paul and Mick were bumping fists, trying to be stoic in the face of their own fear. She saw Robin Daniels talking into his microphone, broadcasting live, his engineer Logan with his eyes closed, obviously wondering why all this was his problem. Her hand found Dave's, and he managed a smile back at her. It was a smile with hardly anything to it, but he'd found it for her.

They reached their objective, a cluster of trees by the side of the road, between two of the posher houses, the big automatic gates of which had remained resolutely shut all night. Wow, those curtains must be setting some sort of record for twitching. Dave looked quickly around with an experienced eye, then squatted down and said something in the language of the gnomes. The voices that replied in the same tongue seemed furious, defiant. Even if Loz couldn't understand the detail, she knew they weren't willing to listen to whatever Dave had said. So he tried again, sounding desperate. Loz could see that he'd begun to cry, but there was something in his determination that didn't acknowledge the tears, just accepted them. It was that same soft power she'd seen from him in all the years she'd known him. She remembered him once getting passionate in the pub with the councillors on the subject of rural homelessness, because the weekend before Lychford's first beggar of the twenty-first century had passed through the town. While some of the others were tutting, he'd said they didn't know what it was like, and that they should try it, not knowing when and how you were ever going to find a home. His eyes had gleamed in the same way then. Now she knew why he'd felt like that, apart from his natural compassion. Here was someone who'd once been very scared, but instead of letting the fear make them want to hurt others, had turned it into an enormous instinct to protect. He was such a looker-after, such a . . .

She found that she'd made an enormous decision. A

decision that wasn't any great development compared to how she'd felt for so long, but one that definitely accelerated things... well, quite a lot. She put a hand on Dave's shoulder to stop him talking, crouched down by his side, and shouted into the undergrowth. "Hey! Hey, listen to me! I can sort this!" She took a deep breath. "I want to marry Dave and have his children, and I'll name them all 'Kev'!"

Dave looked to her, startled. "It won't help if we lie to—"

She kissed him. He kissed her back. The sudden, desperate passion of the kiss Loz hoped would convince their audience, even if her words hadn't. She realized that some of the crowd were actually jeering them, making jokes at their expense, as if they were that hated an enemy now. She didn't care. Her fingers brushed away his tears.

The sound of a voice from the trees made them stop. This time it was speaking English. "They... don't *all* have to be named Kev." From out of the bushes stepped the gnome king, with the gnomette beside him. "Just the first one. You could name the second one after me."

"Whatever it takes," said Loz. "We can start now if you want."

"Now, hold on," said the gnomette, raising a warning hand. "Nobody wants to see that."

"I meant—"

"Will you marry me?" said Dave.

"Yes, that," said Loz, aware she was blushing. She looked to Dave. "That was what I meant. And yes."

"Well, this is one of the three issues resolved," said the king. "This is something we could take to those in our ranks who are keen for this battle to go further."

"We can't do much about the garden gnomes except try to persuade people," said Dave. "We can't order people to comply."

"Then—" The king sounded like he was about to say something doomy and full of regret.

"But with your help, we think we can fix the memorial," said Dave, and he started to tell them about Lizzie's idea. At no point as he did so did he let go of Loz's hand.

After he'd finished, the king let out a long breath. "We could do that. Your man Paul is a decent builder, though some of his joist work is dodgy. And I think two and a bit out of three would convince my people we'd done enough here. But we don't have long. The radicals in my court have that deadline of midnight in their heads now. I can stop the charge to the monument right here, but the squads all over town are planning to have another go at your buildings if we don't get this sorted in time. We can't live with the discord this memorial causes."

"Hey," said Loz, pointing at Dave and suddenly realising she was having her second bright idea of the night, though this one wasn't as potentially life-changing. "What about your trowel?"

"The golden trowel," said the king. "Of course. You'll have it with you?"

"Err, back in a sec," said Dave. And he sprinted off.

Loz managed her most diplomatic smile to the king and gnomette. "So . . . what if our firstborn is a girl?"

The gnomes looked puzzled. "Surely," said the gnomette, "Kev is a lovely name for either?"

"Oh," said Loz. "Great."

Lizzie took a deep breath for three seconds, held it for three seconds, and let it out for three seconds. As she did so, she imagined, with each set of three, bricks forming into a pattern. She breathed and breathed and breathed life into what she saw in her mind as a bridge. Beside her, Autumn and Zoya were pulling power from the air with their hands, each flowing gesture smoothly leading to the next, muttering under their breath as they did.

Across the way, both sets of protestors seemed to dimly perceive the bridge forming. They started to throw stones, but they either went through what Lizzie was imagining or . . . no, no, now they bloody well bounced off it.

Paul, his eyes wide, cleared his throat and put one foot on the bridge, included in the spell that was being worked around him and thus able to see what he was about to start out on in every detail.

"You know what they say," said Mick, "you cross that bridge now you've come to it."

Dave and Loz ran up to them, back from their mission, Dave clutching a slightly chipped and dusty golden trowel. "Took a mo to find it," he said. "It were under a sack."

"And we're engaged," said Loz.

"Oh," said Lizzie, boggling more than a little. "Congratulations."

The alarm went on Lizzie's phone, indicating they had a minute left before midnight. "Go!" shouted Autumn, her face contorted with the effort of the spell.

Dave leapt onto the bridge, a thing that looked so real, and yet faded at its edges and didn't quite touch the ground it was meant to be standing on. But Lizzie didn't care, she'd thrown all her concentration into it, and she wasn't full of anxiety now, she was going to get this done. With a little yell that was half hope and half fear, Paul started forward and Dave ran beside him. "They've got seconds," said Loz.

Robin Daniels ran up to them, his sound engineer Logan behind him, still evidently broadcasting live. "What

I'm seeing here, it's impossible to put into words—"

"You'd better give it a go," said Mick. "It *is* radio."

"—yes, thank you, it's a psychedelic bridge joining what's here to . . . it's going over or past or even through the protestors, getting Paul and Dave to—and they've made it, they're at the war memorial, but we're now down to the last few seconds before the town goes up in smoke! Three . . . two . . ."

Lizzie saw Paul make frantic gestures in the air. Dave flashed his trowel, faster than the eye could follow, and—

As the sound of the church clock striking the chimes of midnight resonated across the town, something else did too. Lizzie had been watching the war memorial, and she'd seen only the slightest of visual shifts, one version of the edifice overlaid on the other. And now maybe it was angled an inch or two differently, but the effect . . .

Something was suddenly more peaceful all around them, more ordinary. The protestors' shouts dwindled into confusion and muttered questions. Lizzie realized she could hear the breeze in the trees.

"Good job," called Paul, giving a thumbs-up signal. He beckoned for them all to come over.

Dave was looking in wonder at the trowel. "I never let it really go for it before," he said. "Not at full speed like that."

"Well, you should," said Loz, "after all this good advertising."

Lizzie saw that the whole crowd had gathered around, looking at the war memorial. "None of the lettering has changed," said Jim. "I thought they wanted to rewrite all that."

"Oh, I have a big explanation about that," said Autumn. "Because, you know, we took the trouble to find out what was actually going on before we formed a mob and made torches." Not hiding her anger, she gave them a condensed version of it.

"Well," said Sheila, after Autumn had finished. "I thought it would all turn out to be nothing much really."

"No you didn't," said Zoya. "You wanted to *burn* us."

"I was obviously under some sort of spell, which whatever you just did has fixed."

Zoya said something in Ukrainian which Lizzie felt was almost certainly a swear word of a particularly serious nature.

"Moving swiftly on," said Lizzie, "something does feel different. What is it?"

Autumn went to touch the war memorial. She closed her eyes for a moment. "It's a feeling made into stone," she said. "It's saying to me that Lychford is . . . a special place that everyone should work together to share and protect."

"My gift to you, in restitution," said a voice from nearby. Lizzie turned to see the gnome king step from the bushes. "I sang the song as young Paul here thought the plans and younger Dave here did the build. I made the memorial sound right for us, so our community isn't continually aggravated by it, but I made it better for you and all."

Lizzie could hear that there were still a few members of the crowd willing to shout things at the gnome about going back to where he came from, so it wasn't as if the magic spell Sheila had decided had been the cause of her bigotry had really been in place and had now been magically fixed. This feeling coming from the memorial was more like a reaffirmation of what she and her friends had always felt about Lychford.

"I'm . . . I'm getting loads of you messaging me saying this was all a prank, a hoax," said Robin Daniels, looking aghast at his phone. "In fact . . ." He scrolled frantically. "I can't find a single one of you who's on Team Believer about this place, but, people, listen, please . . . I *know* what I saw!" He gave Autumn a surprisingly wise grin and headed off, Logan, shrugging, following.

"I think," said Autumn, "his listeners got the sound of the new memorial amplified, and they're all now busy protecting Lychford by saying this was all a fake."

"There goes the tourist trade," said Loz. Who then

looked irked when that got a cheer from the crowd. "Oh come on."

"That was the plan," said the king. "If you stay away from the house we burned for the next three days, you'll find it returned to its previous state. Well, better, to be honest, because it needed a lot doing." He took a step toward Jim, who backed away. "I hope your council will come and visit us. See us. Understand us. I regret that this was how it all went. But if you lot want to live with others, you need to learn how to listen."

Jim didn't seem able to muster a reply. After a moment, the king seemed to realize he wasn't going to get any more satisfaction here and headed back into the bushes.

The crowd slowly began to disperse, some of them with looks of regret, some of them as if they'd just enjoyed a weekend of potholing. "It was good to meet their leader," said Matt Coomby. "I'll see about creating a committee to take him up on that offer, maybe start talking about a twin town project."

"You did well to come out here," said Zoya. "You let them know that not everyone is a wanker."

Matt looked seriously back at her. "I like to think that goes with being on the council."

Jim still looked angry, but his expression now carried with it a hint of despair. "You just did what they wanted," he said. "That's giving in to terrorism."

"No," said Lizzie, "it's making fellow locals feel welcome." And she managed to keep eye contact with him, and she managed to build a determination as strong as her bridge had been until he turned, shaking his head, and headed home. She sighed. "This is going to take so much clearing up."

"Tomorrow," said Autumn, taking her hand. "Everything can begin tomorrow."

Lizzie couldn't look at her. "Oh," she said, "if only that was true."

Epilogue

OBVIOUSLY, THE TOWN COUNCIL had to have an Extraordinary General Meeting about all that had happened. It had seemed, under the circumstances, the least they could do. The Chair, Carrie Anne Christopher, had begun with an address noting for the minutes that she was terribly sorry for not having been present during the unfortunate events in question. "I mean, I pop off to see my aunt for an evening and by the time I get back the town is burning down," she had said. "It's all terribly unfortunate."

That was important, Autumn had thought (she, Zoya, and Lizzie having had their presence requested as witnesses to everything that had happened), that all this had been only the actions of one night. And certainly from Carrie Anne's perspective, what had only been one night had sounded in that meeting like it could be repaired with just a bit of common sense and hearty engagement on all sides. Autumn had even been starting to think that would be the consensus view, until Jim had got up to speak.

"Mistakes were made," he'd begun.

"Yes, you made them," said Sunil.

"Absolutely," said Matt Coomby. And the chamber had erupted with everyone again taking sides. Jim had started to shout that he and those like him would indeed defend Lychford, as the war memorial had "always said" they should, and they could best do that by keeping their garden gnomes in their gardens, indeed adding to them, so those who watched them jealously from other realms would know they stood firm and free. Dave the Mayor had started to yell back that those were his people Jim was talking about.

Autumn had looked at Lizzie and had seen on her face that expression she'd often worn lately, an empty mask that spoke of so much unreachable hurt inside. Autumn had stood up then and had indicated for the other two to do so as well. "We're out of here," she'd told the meeting. "Next time you need us to save your arses, you know where we are."

Which had resulted in a sudden silence.

She'd seen Loz give a little smile at having to enter "arses" in the minutes.

In the weeks that followed that meeting, Dave and Matt

Coomby had indeed led a party of councillors, including Carrie Anne, Sunil, and the now repenting Jackie Parker, to the Land of the Gnomes. They'd returned with a glee that resembled nothing more than them having been on a coach trip to see *The Lion King*. Autumn had noted, however, that they hadn't stayed the night.

When Dave and Loz had had the banns read in Lizzie's church, announcing their forthcoming marriage, Autumn had been there to cheer them on. Indeed, Lizzie had said afterwards that she'd never seen a congregation give such a reading a standing ovation. So there were some parts of Lychford, perhaps the majority, who actually did appreciate all that Autumn and her friends had done. She'd resolved to keep that in mind.

As the nights grew longer, that moment of applause had indeed given Autumn some hope to think back on. And yet the look on Lizzie's face had remained. She had seemed to retreat further by the day. Autumn had had no idea how to reach her. And, given how swiftly she had seen, in this new world of anxiety, how the personal could become the horrific, that lack of connection worried her more by the day.

In the first light of dawn after what the locals had quickly started calling "The Night of the Gnomes," Zoya Boyko had run up the drive of Nanny Louise's house to find Luke exhaustedly opening it for her. "She's safe," he'd said. "Good nanny you've got there. Can I get home now?"

Zoya was not one for hugs, but she'd given him—and then as she'd gone inside, Louise—a look which she hoped had conveyed the strength of her love for the two of them for having stayed strong for her daughter. Louise, still with a gentle smile on her face, had silently pointed to behind a chair, where Zoya had found Jas, playing *Minecraft* on Louise's tablet. Jas had looked up at her carefully, then back, not sulking, just being herself, herself with worries. That autistic stoicism always reminded Zoya of her own character, that way of just getting on with things. "Hello, Mummy," Jas had said.

"Hi," Zoya had replied. "Luke texted me and said things got bad here."

Jas had nodded urgently, without looking away from her game.

"Was it okay in the end?"

"Yeah. Will the gnomes come again?"

"No."

"Will something like that happen again?"

Zoya had taken a moment. She'd already decided upon the sort of thing she'd been going to say, but faced with it, she'd hesitated. But again, that practicality. "Probably," she'd said, very gently, "but we don't need to be scared, because like always when worrying things are coming along, we can talk about it first and prepare."

Jas had nodded fiercely once more.

"Luke said you did magic."

"Sorry!" Jas had looked so worried in that moment.

"No, no." Zoya had smoothed her hair. "It's time for you to learn, so when bad things happen you aren't just making it up as you go but can do more to help. Is that okay?"

Jas had said that it was. And a few minutes later, as they were saying goodbye to Louise, she had finally smiled.

Lizzie had gone to see Owen Trafalgar with what she'd felt at the time was unseemly haste. She'd been surprised to find that the Station Inn was open for business on the very next night after the gnomes had attacked. "We can't close when something awful's happened," said Owen, offering her tea in the small apartment he kept above the pub. "No more than you can."

"Is anyone down there?"

"Paul and Mick of course. A couple of the other regulars. But more will come in as they need to talk."

"I wanted to keep the church open today," Lizzie had begun. "It's just that I have volunteers, not employees, and a lot of them are old, and terrified, and—"

"You don't have to explain," Owen had said. "Oh God, look at you, you're shaking." He'd led her to a chair. The mug had felt wonderfully warm in her hands. "So," he'd said, "there's a woman you're attracted to—"

"And she doesn't feel the same way. Obviously. And this isn't some grand romance that's going to play out, she really doesn't, she's so happy with her husband, and he's great, and I can't tell her, and they're planning to have a baby, and she's *going to have everything I haven't got!*"

The last of that had burst up from somewhere inside her with a force that had startled her, those words which she'd never even allowed herself to put together in her head, not quite, and she'd found herself sobbing uncontrollably.

Owen Trafalgar had taken her in his arms and held her, as she'd just about managed to put down the tea. "Oh," he'd said after a while. "You have *so* not taken care of yourself."

"I can't talk . . . to my best friend," she'd managed to splutter. "I can't tell her."

"Do you really think she'd hate you? Do you think she'd reject you?"

"No, of . . . of course not. She'd be . . . great about it.

It'd just be . . . awkward."

"Wow. Is 'awkward' really worth this? 'Cos if you told her, then you could get on to the jealousy bit and get rid of that too. It's the old story, right? You want her and you want to be her. I remember a bit of that from when I was working everything out."

"How old were you?"

"Really quite a bit younger than you are."

"This is ridiculous. I'm the counsellor."

"I'm a landlord. Same sort of thing."

"But here I am, at my age—"

"Realising you're a bi vicar and having nobody to help you. Except you do."

Lizzie had cried a lot more then and had offered to help in return if Owen ever needed to talk. He'd told her he wasn't religious, and she'd said angrily that that had never mattered, that that wasn't what she was here for, and he'd said okay, okay, and Lizzie had told him about every single female celebrity she'd ever had a crush on, and they'd talked for hours and ended up laughing.

She'd gone home still not feeling entirely right, because the anxiety was still in her body, but . . . she had started to be resolved to do something about this. She would talk to Autumn. After Christmas. Because she needed to get past that enormous annual hurdle first.

And so it came to pass that, in late November, Lizzie was called upon to officiate at two weddings in her church, back to back, one of which had taken longer to organize than the other. Winnie and Brandon, the couple who'd arrived on her doorstep and stressed they wanted no weirdness at their wedding, had gone first. And indeed there had been no weirdness at their wedding. Every time in the last few weeks that they'd come in for a meeting or rehearsal, they'd remarked on how... normal the town seemed now, if a bit... tense?

Lizzie stood now in the porch of her church, her choir and churchwardens busily tiding up for the next wedding, waving at the happy couple as their friends and family saw them off and started getting into cars, heading for the reception.

She waited until the last of those cars had gone around the corner. Then she took a step out into the churchyard and called out, "Okay, you can all come out now!"

From the bushes, and from one of Autumn's magically created invisible bits of space, and from a swish car that materialised at the bottom of the path, and okay, from the coffee shop across the road, a much more Lychford sort of wedding party started arriving. Amongst it was Dave, looking very nervous in his suit, his golden trowel on a chain at his waist, his mayoral chain of office around his neck. Paul and Mick came with him, looking somehow like they'd already spent the night in their suits. From the town itself came the councillors who'd been invited, and from the other realms, out of that invisible patch and in that car, came representatives of many of the other races that bordered Lychford. They'd been told to put on all their pomp and diplomacy, to come and be friendly.

And taking their place beside Dave were the king of the gnomes and the gnomette. Autumn had guaranteed their safety, and Jim, when asked about that, had angrily said of course they wouldn't be accosted by any of his people, but what the ordinary citizens of Lychford might or might not do—

Which had meant that Autumn had taken some extra preventative measures.

To have elf ambassadors at a wedding was quite something. They walked into the church making gestures of protection against a faith which had, back in the day, not been kind to them. They shone, and their light made everyone feel at peace. As soon as the organist hopefully struck up a really pretty close approximation of Wagner's wedding march, and everyone, notably Dave, turned to look toward where the bride would enter, the elves switched off their light, because elf ambassadors were actually getting pretty good now at reading the room.

They were going to need so much of that in the future.

Lizzie watched as Dave's smile grew broader, as Loz, in an enormous and magically enhanced bridal gown, entered the room. Lizzie waved her hands in the air as she sometimes had to do to tell people it was okay, and everyone started to applaud. She saw Autumn amongst those applauding, Zoya and Jas beside her, and she managed the first genuine eye contact and smile she'd had with her old friend in weeks.

They had actually got a chat and catch-up scheduled. Just after Christmas.

Loz reached the altar, her dad on her arm. "Kev, eh?" the old man said to Lizzie, one wry eyebrow raised.

"It's a small sacrifice to make," said Lizzie as she looked between the faces of the happy couple, who were as awkwardly blissful as any she'd seen. "And it preserves the peace. And thank God for that. But hey"—she grabbed Loz and Dave's hands and started to laugh—"spoilers for my sermon."

Acknowledgments

Thanks as always to my wonderful editor, Lee Harris.

About the Author

Lou Abercrombie

PAUL CORNELL has written episodes of *Elementary*, *Doctor Who* ("Father's Day" and "Human Nature"), and many other TV series. He's worked for every major comics company, including his creator-owned series *I Walk With Monsters*, *The Modern Frankenstein*, *Saucer Country*, and *This Damned Band*. He's won the BSFA Award for his short fiction, an Eagle Award for his comics, and a Hugo Award for his podcast, and shares in a Writers Guild Award for *Doctor Who*, and the Grand Prix Nova and Scribe Awards for the audio series *Tom Clancy's Splinter Cell: Firewall*. He's also the winner of the Terrance Dicks Award for lifetime achievement in *Doctor Who* writing. He's the cohost of *Hammer House of Podcast* and *Telefantasy Time Jump*.